## The Claw

"Oh Rache," Kelly whispered. "Something is loose in here. Something big, with fur. And claws." She held out her hand and felt Rachel grab onto it. She felt about four years old, but also a little safer for the human contact. This only lasted for the brief moment until they heard the growling begin. Not a roar. This was more of a sliding sound, a deep growling coming from somewhere in the animal. But not necessarily its mouth, more from deep inside, more of a vibration emanating from the animal, reverberating off the tiles of the room, coming from everywhere at once.

Kelly felt a thin hot trail of sweat running down her temple. The vein in the temple throbbed. "We're done for," she said in a low voice to Rachel.

Look out for:

*Vampire's Love 2:*
  *Blood Spell*
Janice Harrell

*The Stalker*
Carol Ellis

*Point Horror*

# The CLAW

## CARMEN ADAMS

■ SCHOLASTIC

Scholastic Children's Books,
Commonwealth House, 1-19 New Oxford Street,
London, WC1A 1NU, UK
a division of Scholastic Publications Ltd
London ~ New York ~ Toronto ~ Sydney ~ Auckland

First published in the US by Scholastic Inc., 1995
First published in the UK by Scholastic Ltd, 1996

Copyright © Carol Anshaw, 1995

ISBN: 0 590 13970 3

Printed by Cox & Wyman, Reading, Berks

10 9 8 7 6 5 4 3

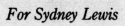

*For Sydney Lewis*

# Chapter 1

"Did you get anything in the mail today?"

This was the first thing Kelly Reade heard when she picked up the phone. No "hello"? Of course, there was really no need for that sort of formality. She and Rachel McFarland had been best friends since fourth grade — since before it was cool for white girls and black girls to hang out together in their small town, Danube, Illinois. They could still remember the days when they got strange looks from some people, when they just had to be determined not to care. It was those early days that had bonded them together. Even way back then they had known they were friends for life.

And it had proved true. Now they were between their junior and senior years of high school and were still best friends in spite of the million differences between them, starting with Kelly being white and Rachel black, Kelly being one of the tallest girls in their class and Rachel one of the shortest. Kelly had the longest (crimped) hair while Rachel always kept hers short. Kelly's favorite food was a big cheeseburger while Rachel was a strict vegetarian. But the one big thing they had in common (besides liking each other a lot) was that they were both ultrasensible. They were never late for school, and they got tons of baby-sitting jobs because they were so reliable. Their rooms were never messy. (Kelly even had her CDs alphabetized by artist.) They took a lot of kidding from their friends for these straight-arrow traits, but their sensibility also created another bond between them.

They always recognized each other on the phone. How could there be any need to identify themselves? All their conversations were really just a continuation of the same, long talk they had been having all these years.

"I just got in," Kelly said to Rachel's question about something special in the mail. "Haven't had a chance to look yet. Wait." She dashed from the kitchen to the front hall, where the mail had been pushed through the slot in their old-fashioned front door and was scattered around on the floor. Some of the corners of envelopes had been bitten by her dog, Noodle, who hated the mailman and so — by dog logic — thought it was important to eat the mail he delivered. Kelly found the envelope she was looking for. Its return address read *Creighton Gardens Zoological Park*. She ran back to the phone, tearing open the slightly munched envelope.

"It looks like I got the internship at the zoo," she told Rachel. "I can't be one hundred percent sure because quite a bit of this letter got snarfed up by Noodle, but I can still read the first part and it says they're pleased to inform me, which must mean I got it."

"I got one, too," Rachel said. "When you think about it, it's pretty incredible — what with all the science nerds, and premed types, and just in general animal lovers who want to get in every summer — that both you and I made it."

"How many do they pick?"

"Only six," Rachel said. "They enclosed a list of their names and phone numbers with the letter. I don't recognize any of them. They must go to Stanton. We're for sure the only ones from Osborne. I don't care, though. We're going to have so much fun, Kel."

"I hope so," Kelly said, trying to sound excited. And she *was* excited, but mostly about getting to work with her best friend. Rachel was the world's biggest animal lover. Given the choice, she would pick animals over people any day. She even wanted to be a veterinarian. Kelly's feelings on the subject were more mixed. She liked cute little pets like Noodle and their cat, Marilyn Monroe. Bigger animals, though, frightened her. She cried once when her dad tried to put her on a pony. And at the circus, she thought the elephant was going to crush its trainer. She was hoping the experience at the zoo this summer would bring her closer to animals, and to being less afraid of them. She hated being prey to stupid fears. It wasn't sensible.

Not all their friends shared their excitement.

"I don't get it," Jessica Freed said in the school lunchroom the next day. "Who would want to work at Creeping Gardens?" A lot of people around Danube referred to Creighton Gardens by this nickname on account of its crumbling, decrepit, overgrown look. The poor old zoo was undeniably in need of repairs and sprucing up. There were always articles in the paper about this, and fund-raising drives by groups hoping to better the conditions there, but things never seemed to change. If anything, the zoo's situation seemed to be getting worse. There was talk lately of closing the place down entirely and moving the animals to some modern, well-funded, big-city zoo that could better provide for them.

"Yeah," said Linda Eaton, as she took her lunch — pizza slice, carton of milk, brownie — off its tray. Linda was another regular at their lunch table. "That place gives me the whim whams. All that moss and those vines and smelly animals pacing around in dark cages. Rrrrr." She made a shivering gesture with her arms and shoulders.

"We don't care about superficial stuff like that," Rachel said, going on the defensive, speaking for both herself and Kelly. "We're not scared off by a little moss. We've got deeper values, like how it's going to be cool just getting a chance to hang out with the animals, getting to know them and all."

"Oh, right," Jessica said. "Hug a mangy camel. That's my idea of fun, all right."

Kelly hated how sarcastic Jessica was being, but she didn't say anything. She could feel Rachel's glare boring through her from across the table, urging Kelly to take her side in the conversation, but the truth was she also thought the zoo was a scary place. Her only hope was that once she got more familiar with it, the scariness would wear off.

"Boy, you were a big help in there," Rachel

said as they tossed their garbage on their way out of the cafeteria and headed off to French class together.

"Sorry," Kelly said. "I wasn't quick enough on my feet, I guess."

"But you *are* happy we got the internships?" Rachel prodded her.

"Of course," Kelly said, trying to sound more enthusiastic than she was. "It'll be cool." She wished she believed this more whole-heartedly, but something about the job nagged at her. She was very intuitive, almost psychic sometimes. And right now her intuition was telling her there was something weird ahead in this summer at the zoo.

Confirmation of this feeling came a week later, the night before she was to start work at the zoo. It was late — eleven or so. Her parents were already asleep. She was up watching TV in the den when the phone rang. She lunged across the sofa to get it before it rang a second time. She was sure it was Rachel with some last-minute question, probably about what she should wear tomorrow. Kelly didn't want her parents to wake up and pick up their extension. They already thought she spent too much time on the phone, *and* that she stayed up too late, so this would raise two sensitive issues.

She was so sure it was going to be Rachel that she just started off saying, "So? What's your problem?"

The voice that traveled back through the line at her, though, was not that of her best friend. Nor of anyone she had ever heard before. It wasn't even a real voice, more a metallic whisper, hoarse and high-pitched at the same time. What this voice said was, *"Problem? I have no problem. It is you who has the problem. That is, if you come to work at the zoo. My advice is stay away. Girls can get hurt in zoos."*

And then there was only the click of the phone being hung up.

"Who was that?"

Kelly jumped at the sound of her father calling from upstairs.

"Was that call for you?"

"No," she shouted back quickly. "Just a wrong number."

Her hand was still on the receiver as she told the lie and felt a shiver run up her arm, as though the phantom caller was still out there somewhere, warning her, waiting for her, plotting some harm. But what? And why? And *who?*

7

# Chapter 2

"Plus it was the *way* they said it, in this totally twisted voice."

Kelly was relating the ugly phone call to Rachel as they drove over to the zoo for the first day of their internship. She tried to imitate the raspy, gravelly whisper the caller had used.

Rachel pulled to a stop at the light at Main and Sycamore, put her car — an ancient yellow Chevy Nova — into neutral. The transmission ground to a halt. Although this car had no first gear and part of the floor missing on the passenger side, it was Rachel's pride and joy. She had saved up two years' worth of baby-sitting money to get it, and bought it the week of her sixteenth birthday. To her and Kelly, it was more than a car, it was wheels — freedom.

While they waited for the light to change,

Rachel turned to Kelly and said, "You say 'they.' Was the voice male or female?"

"Couldn't tell. Whoever they were, they were whispering. Maybe they were trying to disguise their voice. Maybe they were trying to sound creepy. If that was the point, it sure worked."

"Sounds like sour grapes to me," Rachel said, going into her practical mode. "Someone who didn't get an internship and thinks if they can get us to quit, then they'll get the spot themselves or something. Just ignore it. I would if it had happened to me."

Kelly nodded. "I didn't tell my dad when he asked. I knew he'd make me give up the job on the spot. After what's been happening with Heather." Kelly's older sister had run away a few months before and since then her parents had been overly protective of Kelly, as though she might disappear, too. "But do you think whoever it was means real harm, or is just bluffing?"

"Oh, just bluffing," Rachel said — a little blithely Kelly thought.

"How can you be so sure? What if the call was a real threat?"

"Then we'll get other clues. We're not going to go away just because someone makes one creepy phone call, are we?"

"I guess not," Kelly said.

As she spoke, the Nova was turning off the street and pulling through an old stone archway covered with ivy and moss. Across the top was old-fashioned lettering carved into the stone — Creighton Gardens. "Well, here we are." The car's tires crunched in the gravel of the parking lot. Once they had stopped and gotten out, Rachel looked over and could see her friend was still troubled.

"Look, we pride ourselves on being hardheads, tough-minded girls, right?"

"Right."

"So we don't let someone scare us off with a phone call."

"No way," Kelly tried to inject heartiness into her voice, and hoped that would propel her into a braver frame of mind.

"But we'll keep an eye out for any possible weirdness afoot."

"Okay," Kelly said. She still wasn't entirely convinced, but she decided to trust Rachel. Maybe she had been overreacting and a creepy call was no big deal. She decided to put it out of her mind as much as she could.

Their first orientation session was scheduled for nine A.M. Part of their work would involve caring for the animals, but the other part would be acting as docents, roving around one or another area of the zoo, answering people's questions. And so they were going to have to learn about both the zoo and the animals in it, especially the ones in the area they'd get assigned to.

Once they reached the zoo's central courtyard, they easily found Pam Perkins, the zoo's head curator, who was to give them their general orientation. She looked like her name — small and blond and perky. She was dressed in the crisp khaki slacks and shirt that was the Creighton Gardens employee uniform and looked very professional, a perfect role model for a girl thinking of going into zoology. Kelly hadn't thought about it until just this minute, but this was her first real job, as opposed to baby-sitting and mowing the lawn for extra allowance. This was the first time she would have to show up for work someplace and be professional herself. This made her feel a little important, even if she wasn't anything big deal around here, like a zoologist.

Pam introduced Dr. Hoffstadter, the zoo's director, then left while he addressed the interns for a few minutes. Dr. Hoffstadter came from the opposite end of the scientific spectrum from Pam. He looked like the Mad Scientist. Short and fat with stubby fingers. He was unkempt, wearing an old wool suit even though it was June, a tie splotched with several soup stains, thick glasses with lint fuzzing the lenses, and hair in a buzz cut you just knew he'd been wearing for the past thirty years.

"I'm afraid the welcome I extend to you must be a tentative one. This is the third year we've had the summer intern program here at the zoo," he told them, "and I regret to say that due to problems we've had in the past, it is possible this will be the last year for the program."

Everyone in the room grew very quiet. What could they say? Kelly felt as though she were on trial without having committed any crime, without even knowing what the crime was.

Dr. Hoffstadter's mouth scrunched up in a funny way under his unclipped mustache, and then he went on. "Let me just say that I'm not entirely confident that it's a good idea to have such inexperienced young people working with the animals here. Nonetheless, let me welcome you all to the zoo, even if you do turn out to be Creighton Gardens' last summer interns."

As Dr. Hoffstadter was leaving the room, a geeky-looking guy standing next to Kelly said,

"Wow. I mean, what happened last summer, do you think? Somebody paint the turtles?"

"A really nice welcome, wouldn't you say?" said a tall, pretty girl behind Kelly and Rachel as Dr. Hoffstadter left the room, rubbing his hands together nervously and twitching his mustache rather like a demented rabbit.

"I wonder," the girl went on, as if musing to herself, "if the rumors about him are true?"

"What rumors?" Rachel said, turning around to see who was talking.

"Well, they say Dr. Hoffstadter ran another zoo someplace back east, but they let him go for *peculiar practices*."

"Like?" Kelly said. "He talked to the animals like Dr. Doolittle?"

"Well, I can't say this for fact, but what I heard is that at night, the animals roamed free through the zoo, as though it were a jungle, and Dr. Hoffstadter rode around among them on the back of an elephant."

"Oh, right," Rachel said with disgust.

"Where did you hear this?" Kelly asked.

"I heard my father — he's the accountant for the zoo, and he was talking on the phone with one of the board members a few months ago. They were trying to decide how to go about finding out how much truth there was to the rumors." She folded her arms across her chest, as though daring anyone to dispute this gossip.

Kelly immediately pegged this girl as a big-time liar, the kind of person you met on vacation at the beach and she'd right away start telling you about all the movie stars she knew, or how she was a major figure skater. She'd found that these kids also usually had stupid, ridiculous stories about everyone else, too. She just let this sort of stuff go in one ear and out the other. Dr. Hoffstadter was for sure one weird-looking guy, and he didn't seem too happy about the interns being here for the summer, but that didn't make him some nut-cake who waited until the zoo closed for the night so he could ride around on the head of an elephant. Give me a break, Kelly thought.

When she resurfaced from these thoughts and tuned in to what was going on, Pam Perkins had come back and had apparently already met the other interns before Kelly and Rachel had arrived.

"I'm assuming," she said, "that since I've already met the others, that you two are" — she consulted a sheet on her clipboard — "Kelly Reade and Rachel McFarland."

They nodded. Kelly looked over the others

— two guys and two girls. She didn't know any of them.

"I thought we could all take a few minutes to get acquainted," Pam said, leading them over to the gazebo that marked the center of the zoo. "We hold concerts here some nights," she said, gesturing for all of them to sit down in the semicircle of chairs used by the orchestra, "but it's also a good place for informal meetings."

She asked them to go around in a circle and introduce themselves. Rachel went first, then Kelly, then the girl next to her, who was:

"Sandy Lopez. I'll be a senior next year at St. Scholastica. I'm on the swim team there." She giggled nervously. "I don't know what else to say." Clearly Sandy was a shy person, which immediately made Kelly like her, being a little shy herself.

"That was good," Pam said. "If anyone wants to talk about their interests, that would be nice."

Next to Sandy was a thin, nervous-looking guy with an erupting complexion, the geek who'd made the joke about the painted turtles. "I'm Jon Frayne and I go to Stanton High, like Melissa and Griffin," he gestured to the remaining two interns. "I'm interested in science

15

fiction and cars." He laughed nervously at himself. "I feel like I'm applying for a computer dating service."

"It's hard getting to know people at first," Pam said, laughing herself, "even for adults. But we're going to be working together all summer and it's important we feel like a team."

The girl sitting across from Kelly — the liar — was next.

"Melissa Robinson," she said in a slightly bored voice. "I just finished my sophomore year at Stanton and I guess my favorite activities are traveling in Europe and skiing in Colorado."

Kelly looked over at Rachel and rolled her eyes slightly.

The last intern was the one who interested Kelly the most — tall (taller than she was, even) and hunky with hair buzzed short up the sides, long and tangly on top and going to blond at the tips. When he smiled — which he seemed to do a lot — he showed what looked like about two mouthfuls of teeth.

"Griffin Black," he said, introducing himself. "I'm going into my last year at Stanton and I play basketball and write poetry. I'm a big animal lover, especially bears, so I'm hoping I get to work with them here."

Kelly thought she was going to melt into the

floor. He looked and sounded like the guy she'd been waiting for since she'd noticed that boys existed, a few years back. Of course, her noticing him so fast probably meant about a dozen other girls were already in line for him. Girls who weren't so shy.

When Pam got called away to take a phone call, the conversation among the interns again became less formal. It came out in their talk that while Sandy and Kelly and Rachel and Griffin got their internships by applying, Jon and Melissa had gotten theirs through connections. His mother was on the zoo's board and her father was the zoo's financial comptroller and handled all its books. Neither of them seemed particularly thrilled with their internships.

"My mother thinks being here forty hours a week will keep me out of trouble," Jon said, nervously picking at his face, then smirking. "She underestimates me."

"My father says I should learn what it's like to have to work for a living," Melissa said, looking at her perfectly manicured nails as she spoke, as though fascinated by her own perfection. "I don't know why since I don't expect to ever have to work, really, when I get out of school."

"Personally," Rachel muttered to Kelly as

they hung a little behind while Pam led the group off on their tour of the zoo, "I think it would be nice if they gave Melissa the monkey cage cleanup assignment."

"That Jon is a dweeb, too," Kelly muttered back. "Rich kids think they're so great when they really just have more clothes and CDs, which is not the same as being great. Someone ought to point that out to them."

"Rich white kids are the worst—no offense. Melissa informed me that she thought it was 'terrifically enlightened' of the zoo to have hired such a 'racially balanced' mix of interns. Meaning me and Sandy Lopez."

"But why does that make you upset? Maybe she meant it."

"Get real. I can tell. She wanted to sound cool on the issue, but Melissa is one of those people who'd really rather the whole world was white."

"You're being paranoid."

"I'm not. I've developed excellent radar for phony tolerance. Plus I've got a feeling Melissa is a girl who has never said a sincere word in her life."

"She does seem fakey."

"What do you think about Mr. Hunkarama?" Rachel asked, changing the subject.

In reply to this question, Kelly just made a

low whistle. To which a huge tropical bird, whose cage they were passing, came back with its own reply — a loud, piercing screech. Both girls laughed, causing the others to turn around.

Griffin smiled at her and said, "Bet you say that to all the birds."

"I didn't know I was communicating with the wildlife," Kelly said in her own defense. "I'll have to watch what I say from now on. Control my tweets, too."

They toured the primate house, the polar bear pool, the bird house, the big cat house. They talked with the keepers who fed the giraffes and brushed the camels. They met the veterinarians who cared for the elephants' foot infections and the macaws' respiratory viruses, and the veterinarians who supervised the mating of the polar bears. And by then, they were finished with their first day.

"I'll hand out your internship assignments tomorrow morning and then you can get started on your particular area orientations," Pam Perkins said as they were leaving. "Be here at nine A.M. sharp."

Griffin caught up with Kelly and Rachel as they were heading for the parking lot.

"Do you guys need a ride?" he asked, speaking to both of them, but with his hand on Kelly's arm as he said it.

"Uh, well, actually, Rachel has a car," Kelly said, sorry for the first time that she did. If they'd been on foot, they'd be forced to take a ride with Griffin. But from the way his eyes locked with hers as she answered him, she suspected this wouldn't be his last invitation.

*Wow,* she thought. She had only been thinking about this as a summer job, and only really doing it for Rachel's sake at that. And this morning, after last night's weird phone call, she was almost ready to quit before she'd started. Now she was glad she hadn't. Really glad, she thought, as Griffin waved out his window as he drove out of the parking lot.

"Girl," said Rachel, who didn't miss much, "do I see a summer romance on the horizon?"

"He's probably just a flirt. Probably has a dozen girls lined up for that smile," Kelly said. "On the other hand, maybe . . ."

# Chapter 3

"This is great," Kelly's father said after he'd eaten his first bite. Then, after a long, thoughtful pause, he added, "What is it?"

"Greek taco casserole surprise," Kelly said.

"What's the surprise?" her mother asked, a little warily, holding a forkful of her dinner in midair. The whole family was well aware of Kelly's eccentric cooking techniques. "Not M&M's like in that salad last week?"

"No. Just artichoke hearts this time," Kelly said. It was actually she and her sister Heather who had started surprising their parents with weird dinners they concocted as they went along. Kelly's mother and father both worked — her mother as a computer programmer, her dad as an X-ray technician at the hospital. Because of their parents' complicated work schedules, it had gradually evolved that the girls did most of the cooking.

Now, though, Heather was gone. She had snuck out in the middle of the night four months ago and since then the family had been a shell of what it used to be. Kelly knew her sister had become increasingly rebellious and restless. She thought their parents were too strict and conventional. She thought Danube was too small. She wanted to be an actress and knew she wouldn't get anywhere with that dream in a town in the middle of Illinois.

Kelly was the sensible sister and Heather was the wild one. Kelly's big ambition was to go to college and study French literature. Heather wanted to be the star of a TV series. She wanted to party with rock stars, have a house on the beach in Malibu. She felt stuck in high school, in a small town, in a house with people whose dreams were so much quieter than her own.

When Heather had run away, Kelly hadn't been all that surprised, the way their parents had been, but she had been terribly hurt that Heather hadn't told her she was going, or where. It felt like a huge betrayal of all they had shared over the years. And she hadn't made any contact since she'd been gone, either.

She knew Heather had just been protecting herself. If Kelly didn't know where she was, there was no way their parents could wring any information out of her. Still, what Heather had done made Kelly feel totally shut out of her sister's life, and alienated from her.

Her parents were reacting in a different way — bewildered and guilty, wondering what they had done to drive their daughter away, but mostly they were frantic with worry. They had used up a big chunk of their savings hiring a private detective, who so far hadn't come up with anything.

Kelly thought of her sister as extremely capable and take-charge and so envisioned her in total control of whatever situation she was in now. Her parents, though, pictured their lost daughter led astray by creeps, or on drugs, or worse. It had fallen to Kelly to calm their fears, keep them cheered up, and try to fill the shoes of two daughters. And so even on nights when she didn't feel like cooking up something wacky, she did anyway. She tried to act perfectly the part of the sensible daughter, the well-behaved one, the one who was never going to run off and break their hearts.

Which is why she hadn't mentioned the creepy phone call to them. As far as they were concerned, everything about this summer job had to be normal.

* * *

After dinner they watched a video and halfway through the movie, Rachel, who'd had a baby-sitting job that night, came by to sleep over — something they'd done once a week or so since the early days of their friendship.

When the movie was over, the two girls went upstairs and gossiped for a while about who they liked at the zoo (Sandy and Griffin) and who they didn't (Jon and Melissa, especially Melissa), and about how they hoped they would get assigned together the next day to the same part of the zoo.

"We'd better look at those materials Pam gave us today," Rachel said after a while as she opened her knapsack. "Already I can't keep straight everything she told us. I already forget if it's snapping turtles or polar bears that mate for life and how far away you can hear it when a lion roars."

"Five miles," Kelly said.

"Hmmm. Or which are the endangered species."

"Most of them," Kelly said. "We've been encroaching on their territory, using up their space, poisoning their water. They should really be mad at us humans. We've got to do something to turn things around, or most of the species in that zoo will be extinct pretty soon."

"Boy, you really paid attention in that lecture!" Rachel sounded impressed.

"Well, plus I read some of this stuff when I first got home tonight. Hey, what's that?" she said, pointing to a folded-up slip of blood-red paper that had fallen out of Rachel's knapsack onto the floor.

"Don't know," Rachel said, picking it up and unfolding it. As she read it silently, her expression changed completely.

"What?" Kelly said. "What does it say?"

By way of answering, Rachel handed her the opened paper, which contained a short message scrawled in jerky pencil strokes, as though whoever wrote it did it with the hand they didn't usually write with, to obscure their real handwriting — and their identity.

The message read, *Be careful. Don't turn your back on large animals. Cages don't always hold.*

Kelly shuddered and dropped the note to the floor as though it were on fire.

"Who's doing this?" she wondered aloud.

"I don't know," Rachel said, rubbing her hands up and down her arms, as though she had suddenly grown cold. "Someone who wants us out of the zoo, but why?"

"And how far," Kelly added, "are they willing to go to get us out? I don't know about you, but this is much scarier than I was looking forward to in a summer job. I was kind of thinking, you know — easy work, meet new friends, have a few laughs. I wasn't thinking *death threats*. This might be too much for me, Rachel."

"I understand," Rachel said sympathetically. "If you want to quit, I won't try to stop you. Why don't you sleep on it, though? This might not seem so bad in the morning."

But even after they'd shut off the lights and she heard Rachel's breathing even out into sleep, Kelly had trouble dropping off, and when she eventually did, her sleep was tumbled in dreams of deep-growling lions and tigers reaching through the bars of their cages, swiping slowly at her, their claws yellowed and extended, their eyes on fire as they tried to rip her apart.

# Chapter 4

"Sandy — your assignment will be the primate house." Pam Perkins was reading off notes on her clipboard. "Griffin, you'll be in the snack bar in the afternoons and working in the bear area mornings. Jon — report to the bird house. Melissa, go to giraffes and antelopes. Rachel and Kelly, I know you both wanted to work in the big cat house and it looks as though that'll work out, so head on over there and report to Lonnie Bucks."

"All *right*!" Rachel said, enthused.

"Meow," Jon said, making a little scratching gesture with one hand. He was sarcastic about everything. It was beginning to be obvious that he didn't care a thing about animals. He thought they were all just dumb beasts and took every opportunity he could find to point this out. He'd been pressured into the job by his mother, and was determined to be miserable while he was at the zoo and, it seemed, to make everyone else as miserable as he could. After her dreams of the night before, Kelly was in no mood to appreciate his lame sense of humor.

Maybe, she thought, it was Jon who'd put the note in Rachel's knapsack. It *had* been sitting there open all day during the orientation. He could have done it during any of the million moments she hadn't been looking. Of course, any of the others could as easily have planted the note. Or anybody who worked at the zoo, really.

She and Rachel talked about the threats as they walked along the tree-lined gravel path to the big cat house. A storm was coming up. The heavy leaves on the branches above them were whipping frantically in the wind. Kelly had trouble getting the note to stay open so they could reread it.

"I don't know if it's good for you to look at it again," Rachel said. "You might get freaked and decide to quit."

"I'm here today, aren't I? I slept on it and decided you may be right, that I might be overreacting. But admit it, now that you've gotten a threat, you think it's more serious than before, don't you?" Kelly said.

"I'm not sure what I think anymore. For

sure someone is trying to scare us away. Maybe scare everyone away. I guess what I'm thinking is maybe we ought to show this to someone — Pam maybe — and tell her about the phone ca — "

"No way," Kelly cut in. "What's to say she won't tell my parents? And then forget about me keeping this job. They'll yank me out of here in two minutes flat. I'm the only daughter they've got around at the moment and they'd drive me around in a Brink's truck if they could, they're so protective."

"Okay, so we don't tell anyone," Rachel said. Then, after mulling something over she didn't share with Kelly, she added, "Just yet anyway."

The zoo wasn't yet open for the day and so when they got to the back door of the big cat house and wound their way through the narrow, dimly lit tile hallways to the feeding room between the indoor exhibit areas and the outdoor habitats, they knew the man they found there had to be Lonnie Bucks, the keeper of the big cats.

He was middle-aged, tall and lanky, with a jutting jaw and thinned-out hair pasted to his head, and a chin full of whisker stubble that wasn't part of any fashionable look. He was wearing the khaki pants and workshirt that made up the uniform of Creighton Gardens employees, only his weren't so crisp and freshly pressed as Pam's. Everything about him had a sorrowful air.

As they approached, he was bent over a row of large buckets, mixing the meat and supplements for the carnivorous cats' daily meal. And the cats seemed to know it was mealtime. They were pacing back and forth in their runs, hovering around the feeding chutes, making low, menacing rumbles, ominous gargling that sounded, Kelly thought, like drains when they weren't working right.

When Lonnie saw his two new interns approaching, he stood up and politely tipped the billed cap he was wearing, and said, "We feed the big cats out of sight of the visitors. It upsets some folks — you know — to see what the cats do to the meat, how they tear at it with their teeth. Too savage a sight for some."

At first they just stood there in silence at this piece of information, then Rachel, who was by far the more social of the two, said, "You must be our new boss, Lonnie Bucks."

"You'd be right about that," he said, his voice low, with a thick southern accent. He didn't offer anything further. Clearly, conversing with him was going to be like pulling teeth.

"Uh, well, Pam said we should report over here and you'd show us around," Rachel pressed on.

"That would be possible," he said. "But I'm feeding my friends now, as you can see. This here is Ranger; he's a mountain lion, sometimes called a puma. He enjoys cool, dry weather so the summer isn't his favorite time of year, is it, sir?"

For a moment, Kelly thought Lonnie had become more sociable, but then, from the singsong, cooing tone his voice had taken on, she saw that he was really talking to the mountain lion. She then noticed the way the cat looked at Lonnie, and cocked its head as Lonnie spoke. She often talked to Noodle, her dog, and her cat, Marilyn Monroe. But Lonnie's conversation with Ranger was different. It was almost as if he expected the animal to talk back, as if they were having a real conversation. And it was definitely eerie.

She tried not to look as Ranger started in on his dinner, but she couldn't pull her gaze away as he began savagely tearing away at the raw meat with his huge teeth. He didn't look so friendly anymore. She shuddered a little, then hurried to catch up with Rachel and Lonnie.

As they were approaching the lions' habitat, Kelly noticed how feline Lonnie was in his movements. Maybe he had been working with cats for so long that he'd picked up their gestures, become a little catlike himself. Just as she was thinking this, she saw him lick the insides of his fingers, then smooth back the hair at his right temple. Just like a cat. It was so weird, she looked over to see if Rachel had noticed, but she was busy looking over the different feeds for the different cats.

They followed him around the big cat house as he introduced them to all his friends — Madonna and Arnold, the lions, and their cub, Sylvester. Rhett and Scarlett, the tigers. ("Most powerful of the big cats," he told them. "Most beautiful, too. And most dangerous to man.") Then there was Luther, the black leopard. ("Sometimes called a panther," Lonnie explained.) This cat was different from the others. They all looked like giant versions of Kelly's own little cat. But Luther had something else about him, something about his eyes, the way they glowed from within with a scary ice-blue glint. And there was nothing friendly about his expression. Even when Lonnie came up to put his food through the slot, he didn't drop an ounce of his ferocity.

"This is a cat with attitude," Rachel said in a low voice to Kelly.

But Lonnie overheard anyway. He came up and stood behind them and said, "Doesn't like being in a cage. Animals in cages is a sad business. Creatures should have their freedom and this one longs for his. Longs hard." Lonnie looked directly into Kelly's eyes as he spoke.

It was a sunny Monday morning and so the zoo quickly became crowded with kids. Lonnie seemed reluctant to let Kelly and Rachel into the private world he shared with the cats. At the same time he was overworked and glad for the help, especially since — as the girls quickly found out — when interns weren't doing the easy work of being docents, showing zoo visitors around, they were assigned the lowest and grubbiest of zookeeping tasks.

They prepared feed buckets, or were assigned to what Lonnie delicately referred to as "refreshing the habitats," which meant picking up the grounds of the habitats and interior exhibits while the cats were in their runs. Then they hosed down the runs while the cats were shut back in their habitats or exhibit areas.

The interns put down new mulch and twigs and checked to see that the balls and other toys for the animals weren't shredded or mauled, and replaced them if they were. It was hard work. By mid-afternoon, they felt as though they'd been working on a rock pile all day.

Kelly took off her baseball cap, ran a hand through her hair, which was soaked with sweat, and put the cap back on, backward this time. "Now I'm wondering why so many kids wanted this job," she told Rachel. "I mean you'd think they'd have to get prisoners to do this kind of work."

Rachel looked as though she were going to say something, but instead she just nodded and perspired and breathed heavily as she leaned against the handle of her mop. When she was finally able to speak, she said, "Maybe we could teach these cats to clean their own habitats. Then we could go loaf at the snack bar with your new boyfriend. Did he ever get an easy assignment!"

Kelly tried to act indignant. "A, he's not my boyfriend. B, he works with the bears in the mornings and I don't even want to think how dirty a bear habitat can get, and C, *you* were the one who wanted to work directly with the animals," Kelly said.

"Yes, but doesn't it seem to you that we're mostly working not so much with them as with . . . well . . . with what they've left behind?"

Kelly had to laugh.

"I was kind of hoping we'd be able to — you know — pet them or something," Rachel said.

"Are you crazy?" Kelly asked.

"But they're so pretty, so sleek. And the lions are so majestic."

"Right," Kelly said. "And they could swallow your entire head with one little gulp, rip it off with those staple-remover fangs they've got. Did you watch any of them eat their dinners today? We are not talking delicate gourmets. Not to mention the fact that any one of them could tear your face off with one little swipe of its majestic paw. I even got scratched pretty bad by my little cat once when I was teasing her with a dangling ball. Imagine what one of these brutes could do to you without even trying."

Rachel looked at her seriously. "Stop. You're freaking me out. You're still pretty scared of them, aren't you?"

Kelly nodded. "Yeah. But I'm working on it."

Rachel looked back at her, hard. Kelly could see she was trying to be an understanding friend, to respect Kelly's fears even though she didn't share them herself.

"By the way," Rachel said, "Griffin, who I understand is *not* your boyfriend, nonetheless stopped by a while ago when you were off somewhere and said we should stop by after closing. He says if there are any hot dogs and stuff left over, the interns should definitely get them."

And so they went down to the refreshment stand after the zoo's gates had closed for the day.

"I feel so appealing and lovely," Kelly mocked herself, running a hand through her limp, sweaty hair, wiping a streak of dirt off one leg of her jeans. "Griffin is sure to see I'm the girl for him."

"Well, you're not Cinderella. You don't have all those mice and birds to spruce you up and sew you a gown. You'll just have to hope he remembers how you look when you haven't spent the day cleaning up after a bunch of animals."

"Step right up and get your free red hots!" Griffin shouted as Kelly and Rachel came into the refreshment stand. "And I don't think the zoo will go bankrupt if I pour a few extra Cokes either."

Most of the other interns were already there. Sandy was propped on a stool at the end of the counter, telling everyone how monkeys flirt with each other.

"They show off, basically," she said. "The males do anything they can to get the attention of the females. They scratch and screech and dangle like mad from the top of the cage, and you can tell it's all to get the attention of one of the girl monkeys. It's pretty funny to watch."

"Sounds like high school," Griffin said as he worked behind the counter. "I hope you all take the works on your hot dogs."

"Hold the onions on mine," Jon said.

"Hold the hot dog on mine," Rachel said, and laughed.

"Spoken like a true vegetarian," Kelly said.

Melissa had just come in the side door, a little breathless. "Am I in time for those free dogs I heard about?" she said and slipped behind the counter. "Here, I can help, Grif," she said, pulling the spoon out of the mustard.

"Uh, that's okay, Melissa," Griffin said. "Just go around and sit down and relax. You must've had a hard day with those giraffes."

Jon meanwhile took one of the hot dogs Griffin had set on the counter and shoved it into his mouth whole.

"Charming," Rachel said to him. "Remind me to take you with me next time I go to a fancy restaurant."

His response to this was to open his mouth while it was still full of now-chewed-up hot dog.

"Ignore him. Paying attention only encourages infants," Kelly said under her breath to Rachel, but Griffin was close enough to pick up the comment and smile.

"You sound like you've had lots of experience along those lines," he said.

"Just baby-sitting. I'm the baby in my house, and now my sister's gone so I'm sort of an only child."

"Well, if you want contact with little kids, I'll bring you home with me sometime. We have twins at our house. They're seven, but they're about as much trouble as three-year-olds. Maybe you can help me baby-sit sometime. You'd be strict, I can tell."

"Yeah, I'd bring my book on child care," Kelly said, which got him to smile again. It did not, however, raise a smile from Melissa. Instead, her eyebrows scrunched closer together. Kelly felt she was being given the beady eye. Maybe there was already something going on between Melissa and Griffin. They *did* go to the same school. Kelly didn't want to encroach on some other girl's territory. She'd have to find out.

By the time they had eaten dogs and chips and drunk Cokes (Jon burping loudly after finishing his) and talked a while about their first day, it was getting late. The zoo had closed at seven and now it was well past eight.

"Come back with me to the big cat house, will you?" Rachel asked her. "I left my knapsack behind in the feeding room, like an idiot."

"I'll admit there *is* something about the atmosphere of this place that's a little ghostly," Rachel said as they walked back along the tree-lined path. "I think it's all the stone buildings and overgrown vines and heavy trees and all. Makes the place feel a little like a cemetery."

"Yeah, and when it starts to get dark like this, everything turns to shadows, and shadows scare me. I wonder what they're shadows *of*, if you know what I mean," Kelly said.

As they approached the cat house, they could hear the animals pacing and roaming, growling low in some kind of private communication among themselves. Kelly shivered, even though the night air was quite warm.

"I can't find the light switch," Rachel said when they'd pushed open the side door that led directly into the feeding room, which was surrounded by the doors to the cats' runs and habitats.

"It must be right here by the door somewhere," Kelly said, reaching around, slapping her hand along the tile wall.

"Oh-oh," she heard Rachel whisper.

"What?" Kelly said. "Did you find the switch?"

"No. Just a cage door," Rachel answered. "An *open* cage door. And I don't remember any empty habitats. Kel, I think we have to get out of here, and fast!"

But before either of them could make another move, they heard something so close they *felt* it almost as much as they heard it — a low, rumbling breathing, a vibrating guttural sound.

# Chapter 5

"Oh Rache," Kelly whispered. "Something is loose in here. Something big, with fur. And claws." She held out her hand and felt Rachel grab onto it. She felt about four years old, but also a little safer for the human contact. This only lasted for the brief moment until they heard the growling begin. Not a roar. This was more of a sliding sound, a deep growling coming from somewhere in the animal. But not necessarily its mouth, more from deep inside, more of a vibration emanating from the animal, reverberating off the tiles of the room, coming from everywhere at once.

Kelly felt a thin hot trail of sweat running down her temple. The vein in the temple throbbed. "We're done for," she said in a low voice to Rachel.

"Shhh," Rachel said. "If we don't know where it is, it might not know where *we* are."

"Except you know about cats — they can smell better than we can," Kelly said. "And not just us, but our fear. I think our only chance is to get out of here. Maybe if we could just start backing toward the door. Hold our breath and move *very* slowly. We'll just hope it doesn't notice us."

Together, still holding hands out of fear, they began stepping backward. For a while, everything was silent. *Too* silent. And then the space was filled with the most horrific, hideous wail — a long cry that was almost human — as the huge cat lunged through the air. There wasn't enough light in the room to see it, but they could feel it move the air as it sailed past them, thudding to the floor across the room from them.

"Kelly," Rachel said in a shaken voice unlike her usual confident one, "it brushed me with its fur as it went by. It was *that* close."

The cat — they still didn't know which one it was, but for sure one of the big ones — growled again, and this time there was a specific menace to the sound. It was directed toward them. The cat knew where they were now. It only had to pounce and it would have them. One or the other of them. Or both.

"We have to run," Kelly told Rachel, her voice shaking.

"Okay," Rachel replied. She tugged on Kelly's hand as they scurried backward through the room, heading for the thin crack of light coming from the door. They moved faster and harder than they ever had, their hearts pounding inside their chests, their breath burning in their throats as they tried to get enough air.

Rachel hit the door first, threw it open, and the two of them ran out. Kelly looked over her shoulder, expecting to see the cat rushing after them, but the courtyard was empty in the glow of the dim lamppost light. They ran and took shelter behind a partition in front of the door to the women's rest room. From this vantage point, they caught their breath and looked back at the door to the big cat house.

"Why doesn't that damn door close?" Rachel said in a low voice, and Kelly saw what she meant, that it was stuck open about halfway.

And then they both saw it at the same time — the sleek black head and huge shoulders emerging into the light.

"Luther," Kelly breathed, her worst fear materializing in front of her eyes.

The leopard moved fluidly out of the door, stopping briefly to look around, bewildered, into the lighted courtyard — as though astonished at his new freedom. Then for a few moments, he skulked around. So much new space to explore. It appeared that, at least for this brief time, Luther had completely forgotten them.

"We've got to get to a phone," Rachel said in a low voice, but apparently not quite low enough to escape Luther's notice. His huge head whipped around, focused in on the direction of the sound, and in an instant he had sprung across the courtyard in three huge leaps and lunged against the wooden barricade the girls were hiding behind. As he hit the wood with a force that momentarily stunned him, Rachel and Kelly bounced off the partition and ran as fast as their legs could carry them through the corridor between the big cat house and the monkey house, whose back door was, mercifully, open. By now the monkeys inside were screeching wildly with their own fear, as though they could somehow sense the big cat on the loose, as though they were all back in the jungle again.

Once inside, Kelly quickly turned the dead bolt to lock it. Not a moment too soon. She could feel the reverberation run through her hands as the leopard hit the other side of the door. Then, nothing — another moment when the only sound was the cacophony of screeching monkeys.

Rachel said, "The worst part is waiting to see what he'll do next."

They didn't have to wait long. This time they saw him before he hit. He was lunging through the air toward the thick front window of the monkey house. Kelly stood watching as though she were rooted to the floor, unable to move as she watched the huge leopard — its steely blue eyes glaring straight through her, its jaws open, its whole face pulled back to reveal fangs as sharp as stalactites — hit the window with outstretched paws, its claws etching the glass of the window as the leopard fell to the ground.

They were safe! It couldn't get to them. Still Kelly hung back in an aftermath of fear. Rachel, though, ran to the window.

"Quick! He's escaping out the zoo gate! We've got to call security!"

Kelly picked up the phone and dialed 888, the code for security and waited through what seemed like a hundred rings (but was probably only five or six) until she got a guard on the line and related, in a semi-coherent way, what had just happened.

"We'll get on it right away," he promised. "You girls just stay there 'til we come fetch you. Where's Lonnie Bucks anyhow?"

Kelly said she didn't know. "The place was

open, but empty when we got there, and that cage was unlocked."

"But who would do something that dumb?" Rachel said when Kelly had hung up.

"That dumb — or that *evil*," Kelly replied.

With all the security guards racing out of the zoo to try to find the black leopard, who was now on the loose in the town somewhere, Kelly and Rachel's rescuers turned out to be Griffin and Melissa.

"Oh, I'm so glad nobody got hurt!" Melissa said, giving Rachel a bone-crushing hug that somehow seemed false. Maybe she was sincere, but Kelly didn't think so. Kelly tried to give her the benefit of the doubt. She herself was a shy person and knew people often mistook that and thought she was being aloof and haughty.

Griffin didn't say anything, which was more telling about his feelings for Kelly than anything he could have said. His look when he saw her was one of utter relief. And when he came over to her and put an arm around her shoulders, she pressed her face into the hollow of his neck and just let flow all the tears she had been holding back through the whole ordeal. There was no self-consciousness between them. It was as if this horrible incident had skipped them over weeks of tentative flirting and getting acquainted. In this moment of relief, she felt truly close to him.

"It's scary to think if anything had . . ." he started to say into her ear, but she pressed her fingers against his mouth.

"But it didn't," she said.

The intimacy of the moment was ripped into by the syrupy voice of Melissa saying, "What a sweet picture. Like the last shot in one of those old adventure movies. When the hero saves the heroine and kills the terrible beast."

Kelly broke away from Griffin and stared her down and said, "Right, except no one saved anyone and the beast is still at large." She looked up at Griffin and added, in a much softer voice, "And I don't feel like this is the end of anything."

The door flew open and Pam Perkins rushed in. Unfortunately, Dr. Hoffstadter was with her, his hands rubbing each other furiously while his mouth was moving madly, his mustache twitching, his eyes huge behind the thick lenses of his glasses.

"What incompetent fool allowed this travesty of zoological management to happen?!"

Kelly felt her knees begin to shake. She

hated getting yelled at. It made her feel guilty even when she wasn't.

Rachel was much less easily intimidated. "We were in the snack bar when it happened. We only came back to the cat house to get my knapsack. And lucky for everyone that we did. Otherwise that leopard would've been long gone by the time anyone noticed."

Dr. Hoffstadter wasn't about to be stopped by reason, though. His face was deep crimson and he was sweating. "That cage was supposed to be locked!" he exploded. "*And* the door to the big cat house. *And* the side gate to the zoo. Things have gotten too lax around here, far too lax. And someone is going to pay."

"Well, that someone . . ." Rachel started to say, under her breath.

". . . isn't us," Kelly finished, muttering herself. They knew they weren't in the wrong, but there was clearly no use fighting with Dr. Hoffstadter tonight, what with the fury he was in. They didn't want to lose their jobs the first day.

Pam, who had gone out again while Dr. Hoffstadter was raging, rushed back in now with new, worse news. "This is terrible. The security trucks haven't been able to even *spot*

Luther, much less catch him. He seems to have truly escaped, and who knows what he'll do when he comes across humans who aren't safely on the other side of bars from him!"

Kelly felt a terrible shudder pass through her as she recalled the words of the disembodied voice on the phone. *"Girls can get hurt in zoos."* Maybe elsewhere now, too. Where would a safe place be with a leopard on the loose?

# Chapter 6

"We are certain of capturing the escaped leopard, have no fear," Dr. Hoffstadter was saying to the gathering of all the employees and interns in one of the staff locker rooms an hour or so later. "And beyond that," he said nervously — he said everything nervously — "we are determined to get to the bottom of what *really* happened here tonight. Whoever left that cage unlocked will not go unpunished. We are at present discussing possible suspects with Mr. Bucks, keeper of the big cat house." He gestured toward Lonnie, who had apparently already gone home for the night by the time the girls had returned to the cat house. He was back now, though, and looking quite agitated. Kelly figured that — even with all his talk of how wild animals need their freedom — he was probably plenty upset that one of his cats was gone, and endangering the local citizens.

When Dr. Hoffstadter and Lonnie left to deal with the press, who had been gathering outside, Kelly stood thinking how different he had sounded talking to the larger group of employees. The way he had gotten his anger under control so quickly was almost as strange as the outburst Kelly and Rachel had witnessed earlier. Maybe there *was* something peculiar about him. Maybe Melissa hadn't been spinning a tall tale at the orientation.

Her thoughts were interrupted by the nasal voice of Jon, muttering in her ear about Dr. Hoffstadter. "Poor idiot hasn't got a clue. Doesn't know where that cat is, or who let it out. That's what I like — a guy who's really on top of his job."

"What I want to know," said Melissa, who had slithered up behind him, "is where was Lonnie Bucks when all this happened?"

"That cat man is one weird guy," Jon said to Rachel and Kelly.

"Weird how?" said Kelly.

"Well, doesn't he kind of *look* like a cat?" Melissa observed. Kelly noticed something she'd missed earlier — that Melissa was wearing a tan silk shirt and crisply pressed khakis, an outfit assembled, no doubt, to make her look like a real zoo staff member instead of just a summer intern. Maybe Rachel was right — that there wasn't *anything* about Melissa that wasn't phony, bogus, or fake.

"I didn't know there was a law against that," Rachel said defensively. She kind of liked Lonnie in spite of his undeniable weirdness, and Melissa had gotten her hackles up.

"I myself think the guy has been working a little too long with felines," Jon offered. "He looks like them, probably relates to them better than he does to people. And I've got to mention that yesterday I thought I smelled tuna on his breath."

"Very funny," Rachel said, arching an eyebrow witheringly (she was great at this, Kelly thought) to show how decidedly *un*-funny she thought he was.

"You have to admit that after Dr. Hoffstadter — Dr. Mondo Weirdo, that is — Lonnie is the most likely person to have let that cat out," Melissa said. "Kelly told us that thing he said about animals not being in cages. Maybe he just really started to believe that and went around the bend tonight. Thought he'd give one of his friends a little vacation."

"I don't buy it," Kelly said. "I think Pam said he's worked here like twenty years. Why all of a sudden tonight? Our first day on the job?"

"Just what are you implying?" Jon said.

"I just think this has something to do with us." She looked over at Rachel. They hadn't said anything to anyone so far about either the phone call or the note. Rachel shook her head slightly, which Kelly knew meant not to say anything now about the threats either.

A little later, when they were alone, Rachel explained, "How do we know it wasn't one of *them* — one of the other interns — who made the threats? It's not impossible. I think we just ought to hold tight and see what happens now."

"And it does seem as though something might. About every other person around here seems peculiar enough to be capable of doing all this. What a place!" Kelly said.

"Right," Rachel agreed. "It sure does seem that something's going on at this zoo that's bigger than us. Even bigger than a runaway leopard."

On their way out of the zoo, the girls were set upon by reporters from the daily paper and the two TV stations. They were shouting over each other, jamming microphones in front of the girls' faces.

"Are you the two who were savagely attacked by the tiger?"

"Are you maimed?"

"Is the zoo taking full responsibility for your injuries?"

"There were no injuries. There was no actual attack," Rachel said. "We're fine."

"And it's a black leopard," Kelly said. "And the zoo is confident they will retrieve him." She felt like a spokesperson for the zoo, and after only one day of working there, but the reporters made her feel defensive. Also, she didn't want to show anyone — especially not everyone in town who watched television — just how frightened she was.

Griffin gave them both a ride home. The police had declared a curfew for the night. Until the black leopard was found, they felt the streets weren't safe.

Kelly wasn't even completely through the front door of her house when her parents leaped up from the TV, on which she was astonished to see herself talking to the reporters! Then Rachel was on, then Kelly herself again. She was so fascinated watching her fifteen minutes of fame, she forgot that this was *new* news to her parents, as opposed to old news to her.

And she hadn't realized, as she was talking to the reporters, how the news media would hype the story, how charged it would come across. Nor had she quite realized until this moment that the incident they'd just been through was probably the biggest story to hit Danube, Illinois, in years. This was a sleepy small town. They didn't have big drug busts or serial killers. Fires and car wrecks were about the biggest stories on the local news shows. An escaped leopard would send tremendous shock waves through the town and its residents, particularly the two residents standing in the living room with her now.

"Are you all right?" her mother said, taking her by the arms, patting her head, smoothing her hair, as though she were going to discover some injury under her daughter's seemingly normal appearance.

"I'm fine," Kelly said, and tried to think of a way to downplay what had happened. Her parents were so easily upset since Heather had run away, and she didn't want to stir them up any more than was absolutely necessary. "It was just a little cat and Rachel and I happened to be sort of around." She hoped that sounded distant enough from the actual event.

"*Little* cat," her father snorted. "A leopard."

"And why are those reporters asking if you were mauled if you were so far away when it happened?"

"Those reporters also thought it was a *tiger*. They're totally out to lunch."

"Well, that might be, but you're still going to have to quit that internship immediately. You're not going back to that zoo!" her mother said.

"Why not? Given the speed with which that leopard got out of there as soon as he could, I think the zoo's the safest place in town now," Kelly said. "And now the security will be tighter than it's ever been."

She was totally bluffing. She had no idea what the security around the zoo was like. Clearly it hadn't been all that tight if someone just walked in and let a leopard out of its cage. There was so much about the zoo — Lonnie Bucks and his strange affinity with the cats; Dr. Hoffstadter and the peculiar rumors about him; the ease with which whoever let Luther out was able to do so; the threats, probably from that same person — so much that she couldn't tell them beyond what they'd just seen on TV. It was hard to believe that just a couple of days ago she was looking forward to an easy, fun summer job and now she was enmeshed in a hideous web of sinister activity and deadly mystery. There was no way she could tell her parents even a tenth of what was going on. They would be too upset, and surely make her quit, and now, even after what she had been through, she was beginning to think that she was needed at Creeping Gardens to help sort out whatever was going on. Someone might be after the interns and it was going to have to be the interns who uncovered who this was.

Over the next half hour or so, Kelly was able — with vagueness and generalities — to calm her parents down and get them to let her continue working at the zoo. She was on her way into the kitchen to make everyone hot-fudge sundaes — an old family tradition — when the phone rang.

"I'm up anyway," she shouted into the den. "I'll get it in the kitchen."

When she picked up the receiver and put it to her ear thinking she was about to say hi to either Rachel or Griffin, she didn't even have a chance to speak. She found herself blasted against the wall by an unmistakable sound, one she had heard for real just hours earlier — the loud angry roar of a huge jungle cat. She hung up quickly, her heart racing.

She tried to calm herself down, tell herself it must have only been a recording, made by someone who wanted to terrify her. The problem was, they were beginning to succeed.

# Chapter 7

The next morning, the front gate of the zoo was crowded with reporters clamoring for fresh details. Plus about a hundred people from the town had gathered, demanding to know what was being done to capture the leopard. A few were even carrying signs that read *Zoo great for animals, but what about humans?* and *Close Creighton*.

Kelly and Rachel had to push their way through all of this anger and commotion and repeatedly tell the reporters "No comment" in response to their questions.

Even inside the gates, everyone was nervous, agitated, jumpy. The place was filled with rumor and speculation, all bred out of fear. Fear of the leopard that was still on the loose. Fear of whoever had let it out and what they would do next.

Rachel had a global explanation (her specialty) for the nervousness, which she offered to Kelly and Griffin in the lunchroom. "I think the deal is that zoos are based on a fundamental principle — safety for the humans who come to visit. They want to observe without being bothered by monkeys, pecked by birds, crushed by elephants, and especially without being mauled by big cats. When the safety zone evaporates — the way it did for us last night — everyone gets shook."

"Not to mention the phone call I got last night," said Jon, who had just come into the room and was pushing change into the coffee machine.

"What do you mean?" asked Rachel, for the first time curious about something Jon had to say.

"Some creep advising me to forget about escaped cats. Said what I need to do is watch that old movie, *The Birds*. You know, that old horror flick where everyone is running around screaming because all the birds have turned into evil incarnations or something. At first I thought it was just one of you trying to be funny, but there was nothing funny about this call, if you know what I mean. And it clearly came from someone who knows I'm working in the bird house."

"The voice — was it a man or woman?" Kelly asked.

"Couldn't tell. It was more a whisper. Which made it even creepier." It was evident from his manner — completely devoid of his usual sarcasm — that he had been rattled by the call.

Rachel and Kelly exchanged glances and nodded in silent agreement.

"We've gotten the same sort of threats, too," Rachel said. "Kelly and I."

Griffin and Jon wanted details. Melissa, too. She had come in during the middle of all this and sat down with her doughnut and paper cup of tea. "What is all this? Fill me in."

When Kelly and Rachel had finished telling their stories, Melissa quickly added one of her own.

"The thing is, uh, I was out jogging one night just before we started the internships and suddenly someone came up behind me and grabbed onto the back of my shirt and said — well, they really kind of whispered, but in this raspy way — said I really should think twice about working in a zoo. That the animals might turn on me. It was kind of like in *The Godfather* where they advise you in this fake-nice way, and if you don't listen you wind up sleeping with the fishes. Like that. Anyway it all happened so fast and then whoever it was just ran past me real fast. Plus I guess I didn't really want to catch up with him."

"Wow," Griffin said. "You must've freaked. Did you see who it was?"

"Uh, no, not actually," Melissa said, pulling one side of her sleek reddish blond hair back behind her ear. "Whoever it was was just in a jogging suit. Totally unisex. And they were wearing a cap so I couldn't see their hair. Tall-ish, though. I don't know. Could have been either a man or a woman."

"Well," Rachel said, "that puts us pretty much back to square one."

Kelly thought for a minute. "That means some of us have gotten at least one threat. Sandy hasn't, but by the way, where is she this morning?"

Jon shrugged. "Haven't seen her around."

"Maybe she got freaked by what happened last night," Melissa suggested. "Or her parents pulled her out of the job."

"No, I saw her on my way to work this morning. Rachel, you probably didn't see her because you were driving. She was riding her bike. She was definitely heading in this direc-tion."

"Where exactly was it you saw her?" Rachel asked.

"We were just going by the old, abandoned underpass, as I recall."

"Where's that?" asked Jon, whose family was wealthy and lived outside town.

"About a mile from here, out toward the highway," Kelly said. "Even though it's been closed to cars for years now, everyone still uses it as a shortcut when they're walking or on a bike."

"She really shouldn't have been riding her bike today, with that leopard on the loose," Griffin said.

"My thoughts exactly," Rachel concurred. "And especially not through the old underpass. With all its old nooks and crannies and abandoned tool rooms and stuff, it's got to be one of the creepiest places in town — filled with great, dark hiding places for a black leopard."

"Let's not get hysterical," Kelly said. "Sitting here talking like this, we just wind up freaking each other out. Maybe Sandy got here ages ago and just went straight to the monkey house."

Griffin volunteered to look for her there, but he came back shaking his head. "She hasn't been there yet."

"Maybe she got scared and turned back and is safely at home even as we speak," Kelly said. "I'll call her mother. In case she isn't there, I'll make up something that won't get her all upset."

When Kelly came back into the lunchroom, the others all looked up expectantly.

She shook her head. "Nope. Mrs. Lopez said Sandy was at work. But as you can see we are all at work and she is not. I think we'd better go look for her."

"Well that's very brave of you, but crawling through dark, deserted underpass tunnels with a leopard on the loose, uh, count me out," said Melissa.

"Yeah, well for me the thing is, I hardly know Sandy," said Jon. "Besides, I think I hear my fine feathered friends calling me." He cupped his ear. " 'Tweet, tweet. Come back to us, Jon.' "

"Thanks, guys," Rachel said sarcastically. "I can see that when the going gets tough, the tough get going — fast and in the opposite direction."

"*I'll* come," Griffin said. "We can go in my car, then get out and go through the tunnel on foot. If she's in there, we'll find her."

"Thanks," Rachel said, then, turning toward Jon and Melissa, "and you'd come, too, if you'd been through our little encounter with Mr. Leopard."

"Maybe it's *because* you went through your scary little experience that you're overreacting now," Melissa said.

Jon added, "Yeah, Sandy's probably fine. You're all getting worked up over nothing."

"Yeah, right," Kelly said to Rachel and Griffin when they were on their way to the parking lot, steering their way through the cordon of reporters and frightened and angry townspeople. "They may think Sandy's all right, but all I know is the hairs on my arms are standing straight up."

Rachel nodded. "I know. Something's wrong again. I can feel it, too."

With Griffin behind the wheel and Rachel watching out one side of the car, Kelly out the other, they went back over what it seemed would have been Sandy's most likely route to work. They found no trace of her between the zoo and the underpass tunnel where Kelly had last seen her.

Griffin pulled the car over onto the shoulder. "Looks like we're going to have to go in there on foot. Anyone want to chicken out now?"

Both girls shook their heads, and the three of them — staying close together for an un-spoken sense of safety in numbers — began walking slowly into the old stone tunnel where the road went under the highway.

Darkness immediately fell upon them, and the warm humid day turned into a cool, clammy, instant night. Everything was in shadows. The underpass had been built ages before and was propped up with concrete pillars and, here and there where the structure had become weak, with wooden beams that were by now in some stage of rotting away. In some places water dripped from the ceiling, through patches of rust and furry moss.

"Sandy!" Kelly shouted lightly, and then the three of them held very still to see if there was any reply.

Nothing.

"Sandeeeee!" Griffin tried, using his loudest voice.

Still nothing. But then, when they moved further into the tunnel and Kelly shouted Sandy's name one more time, there was a faint response that sounded like: "Here."

But where was it coming from ? The three of them rushed on, calling out her name, then stopping, then running again.

"Here!" again came the tiny, disembodied voice out of the vast nowhere of the tunnel.

Finally, Griffin said, "Over here!" And off he ran to a nook between two huge concrete pillars where Sandy lay next to her bike, which was bent like a large metal pretzel. She was clearly dazed, and holding onto her arm with her sweater wrapped messily around it. She was looking up at the three of them with only half recognition. The other half of her expression was a wide-eyed fear. She was streaked with dirt everywhere. Her shirt and jeans were torn.

"It's us," Rachel said, crouching beside her, "your friends. Rachel and Kelly and Griffin."

"Are you okay?" Kelly said, also dropping to Sandy's side, and then thought a moment and added, "Dumb question. Of course you're not. But Sandy — what *happened*?"

"I-I-I don't know. Not sure. I was riding my bike — " She pointed vaguely to the opposite end of the underpass, where she would have come in, and then let her hand drop into her lap. "Then something was after me . . ." As Sandy went on to haltingly describe what happened, the whole horrible, hideous scene jumped full-blown into Kelly's imagination.

"I had been riding along on my bike, on my way to the zoo, not particularly nervous about the leopard on the loose. I know what happened to you guys and the TV news is full of it, but somehow it still didn't seem really real to me.

"I was pedaling along at a pretty good clip, wanting to get through the underpass as fast as I could. I've never liked it in here. I always worry it's full of spiders and snakes and stuff — so dark and damp, like a big basement.

"And then suddenly I knew I wasn't alone. I could feel something else in there with me, keeping pace with me, then catching up to me, then brushing past me in the dark. It was something black — I couldn't really see it at all in the darkness — and covered with a sleek fur. I just about fell off my bike in fear, but somehow I managed to keep cool enough to pedal on, as fast as my legs would pump.

"But it wasn't fast enough. In a blur, the creature doubled back, then leaped up off the ground it was running on, and lunged at me with its front claws extended, tearing at my arm, knocking me off the bike. I hit the ground hard and found myself rolling on the old, broken-up asphalt pavement. Vaguely, I saw I was heading for a narrow space where the stone walls didn't quite meet the ground. Miraculously, I was able to roll into this crevice while the animal — and by now I knew it was the black leopard — once again lunged through the air at me, but hit the stone of the wall instead.

"When it got up, I could see the cat was

dazed. It looked around, the blue of its eyes picking up the dim light from the far-off end of the tunnel — flickering as they searched around for me. I held my breath and lay as still as a dead person, even though the very thing I most wanted to do was run through the tunnel screaming, fleeing this ferocious feline.

"After the longest moment of my life, I saw that the leopard had become disoriented, had lost track of me or forgotten he'd been after me in the first place. It sniffed at the air with an upturned head, then ran off down the tunnel toward the other end.

"It was only then that I realized I was hurt. That leopard didn't kill me, but it wanted to. And it left me with *this*."

She lifted the sweater she had been pressing against her wounded arm to stanch the flow of blood. The other three looked down at the hideous sight, Sandy's arm mutilated, etched deeply with five deep cuts running the length of her upper arm. The mark was fresh, a scab was just barely beginning to form over this signature, this warning from Luther.

"Oh, Sandy," Kelly cried, touching her. "This is so horrible."

"You were so brave, though," Rachel said.

"Well, I thought fast, I guess, but I'm not

brave. I haven't stopped shaking since it happened."

"But he's gone now," Griffin said, trying to be comforting as they helped Sandy to his car.

"Oh no," Sandy said, her voice shaking. "He's not gone. He's very much out there . . . somewhere."

# Chapter 8

In the emergency room of Danube General Hospital, Rachel and Kelly and Griffin waited while the doctors worked on Sandy's arm. From beyond the doors to the outside, they could hear the din of reporters and curious residents of the town. Within moments, it seemed, of the police being called, Sandy's story was on TV. The evening paper on the table in the waiting room already blared the headline: LOCAL GIRL MAULED BY BIG CAT *City Cries Out: "Luther Must Be Caught!"* And in smaller type: *Zoo Officials Say Capture Imminent*.

Unfortunately, Kelly didn't need the news media to inform her father of what had happened. Danube General was also the hospital where he worked in radiology as an X-ray technician. When he got wind of what had happened, and that Kelly was down in emergency, he was there in a flash — furious. After extending his sympathy to Mrs. Lopez, he turned on Kelly.

"How could you have let yourself get into such a dangerous situation?" he grilled her. "That damn cat might have still been in that tunnel, and then what? You all could have been killed."

She hated getting yelled at, and the fact that this scene was taking place in front of Rachel and — worse — in front of Griffin, was hideously embarrassing. She could feel herself blushing as her father went on about how irresponsible she'd been.

"I'm sorry," she said, mostly to stop him. "We were just so worried about Sandy."

"This was something for the police to handle, not a bunch of impulsive kids," he said, casting a slightly less angry look in Griffin and Rachel's direction. He was fed up with them, too, but at least they weren't *his* kids.

"I don't want you ever pulling a stunt like that again," he said to Kelly, and then, to show her he was more upset than truly angry, he put an arm around her and pulled her into a hug. She hardly ever saw him in his work clothes — mint-green cotton scrubs — and it made her realize he was a person out in the world, not just her father, which was the only way she usually thought of him. And she could see he was just trying to do the right thing here, in the same way she'd been trying to do the right thing in going back to find Sandy. Somehow, unfortunately, these two good efforts had put them on opposite sides of the fence at the moment.

All her life, Kelly had enjoyed being the good, sensible daughter. Now, in a matter of days, she seemed to have turned into a reckless and daring adventurer. What was happening?

"I'm sorry for upsetting you," she told her father, and this much was true. "And I won't get into any dangerous situations again around this." For this part of her statement, she crossed her fingers behind her back as she spoke. She *might* not get into any more scrapes, but if necessary, she knew she probably would. Because somewhere along the way of receiving the threats and staring at the leopard, she had crossed some line from being afraid, to still being afraid but more being angry at whoever was trying to scare them off. And beyond that, she had become fiercely curious about what was really going on at the zoo, what larger plot they had all been sucked into.

Plus she liked the rush she got when she

was her most courageous self. She wanted to keep this person alive, alive and fighting the forces of evil. It made her feel like someone with a mission, as opposed to someone with a summer job, and A's in French, and good hair.

After Kelly's father had gone back down to radiology, Griffin leaned across from the plastic waiting room chair he was sitting in and took Kelly's hands.

"Hey," he said, smiling that incredible smile of his. "He *had* to do that. He's your father. He had to be concerned and upset and protective."

"Yeah, but he wasn't this bad before my sister ran away. Sometimes I feel like I'm taking all the heat for her bad behavior."

"They're going to find Heather and this phase will all be over," Rachel said, neatly turning a conversation for two into one that included her, too. Kelly was glad that Rachel seemed to like Griffin and didn't mind his being around. There had been other times when one of them hadn't much liked the boyfriend of the other, and those had been rough patches.

"You were lying to him, though, weren't you?" said Rachel, who probably knew Kelly better than anyone in the world. "If this requires more danger, you'll jump in again feet first, won't you?"

Kelly felt a cold, metallic shiver pass through her, but also felt the beginnings of a steely courage forming within her as she said, "Maybe."

Just after the doctor had come in and asked Mrs. Lopez to come with him to see Sandy, Pam Perkins rushed in.

"How *is* she?" Pam asked, a little breathless.

"We're waiting to find out," Kelly said. "Mrs. Lopez is with the doctor now."

Griffin, Kelly, and Rachel described how they had found Sandy, and what shape she had been in. With Sandy's mother out of the room, they could speak frankly.

Pam nodded and seemed distressed, but distracted at the same time. Maybe the whole business with Luther was too much for her to contend with, Kelly thought. Then small tears began to stream down Pam's cheeks.

"Oh, I just hope they find that cat so everyone feels safe again, and the zoo doesn't sink under all the negative publicity. I'm just so frustrated. There was supposed to be an independent audit of the Creighton Gardens accounts starting today," she explained. "But with this leopard on the loose, it's being postponed again — for the umpteenth time, I'm afraid."

How, Kelly wondered, could Pam even care about some stupid accounting procedure when everyone was in so much danger with Luther on the loose?

It was almost as if Pam were reading her mind when she went on, "I want the zoo to survive. The way it's going, zoos are becoming one of the few safe havens for animals that are being hunted to extinction, or run off the face of the earth. We've never had a dangerous animal escape before in the history of the zoo. And I'm sorry one has escaped now. And I feel so terrible about Sandy getting hurt.

"But I have to admit I am also sorry all this is happening at a time when the zoo is in such a precarious position. This is just the sort of thing that will seal its doom, I'm afraid — give its opponents a club with which to beat it to death. 'The zoo is unsafe,' they'll say, and I'm afraid enough people will believe them that they'll just move the animals out and lock the gates to Creighton Gardens forever.

"The audit is our best hope. We never seem to have enough money to pay our basic bills, much less do all the repairs needed around here. I'm supposed to help our comptroller, Mr. Robinson — Melissa's father — gather up all the necessary documentation to give over to the auditors. I haven't gotten it all yet. And now this incident seems to have postponed the audit yet again. It's all very frustrating."

"Pam," Kelly said, "are you and Dr. Hoffstadter and the police looking at the possibility that someone is out to sabotage the zoo?" Even as she was saying this, she was wondering if maybe Dr. Hoffstadter wasn't the one responsible for the sabotage. He certainly was against the internship program. Maybe this was only part of some larger secret antagonism toward the zoo, maybe to all zoos. Melissa had said he was fired from another zoo. Maybe this time she hadn't been lying. Kelly didn't feel safe mentioning all this to Pam, though. As far as she could see, Pam and Dr. Hoffstadter were on good terms. Maybe they were best friends.

"What do you mean — sabotage?" Pam said now, clearly intrigued by the idea.

Kelly and Rachel and Griffin detailed the threats the other interns had received.

"And someone left that cage door open last night," Kelly said. "It could have been an accident, but maybe not."

"Jon and Melissa think it was Lonnie, that he's behind this whole business," Griffin said.

"But we don't," Kelly was quick to add. "Lonnie is peculiar, but he doesn't strike us as sinister."

Pam agreed. "I've known Lonnie since I started here six years ago and he's really very sweet under his shyness and lack of socialization. He wouldn't hurt a fly, as they say. If you're right and someone around the zoo is up to some bad business, it's not Lonnie. I'll guarantee it."

"But who, then?" Griffin said. "Someone opened that cage door. Someone made all those threats."

"Yeah," Kelly said. "And that someone is still out there, on the loose. Like Luther."

# Chapter 9

*CRASH!!* Kelly sat bolt upright in her bed. In her dream the earshattering sound had been a jungle cat leaping off a high branch, the branch cracking off under the pressure of the animal's powerful hind legs as it leaped through the air, down onto *her*.

When she was fully awake and had shaken off the dream, she realized the huge crash had actually been thunder. It was pouring outside her window — and in! She jumped up to shut the window. Noodle hopped off the bed as she jostled him out of his resting place, and scuttled under the bed. He was terrified of thunder and lightning.

She took a shower, then put on clean jeans and a fresh T-shirt and vest. Dressing for work at the zoo was a problem. That is, although she might be doing grunge work, she was also almost sure to run into Griffin (not to mention the TV cameras that seemed to catch her and Rachel every time they came in or out of the zoo), and didn't want to look totally grotty.

She had washed her hair in the shower, then dried it with a towel and worked on it with her crimper for a while. It was still damp when she finished. This was her method — leave it slightly damp and let it fan out as it dried the rest of the way on its own. She knew her hair was one of her best features, that other girls at school talked about it.

When she got downstairs, her mother was already there, reading the paper and having a cup of coffee. She was a computer programmer and worked nights because the overnight shift paid better. She got off at seven and was home by seven-thirty, in time to have breakfast with Kelly. Then with Kelly off to school and Kelly's father at the hospital (he worked seven in the morning to three in the afternoon), she went to sleep through the morning and early afternoon.

Usually Kelly and her mom had cold cereal together, or Kelly made herself a soft-boiled egg, toast, and cup of tea. But this morning her mother was all revved up, scrambling eggs. Strips of bacon were draining on paper towels on the counter. She was clearly agitated, but in a happy way. Kelly was surprised. She had noticed the morning paper on the kitchen table. Today's headline read: LUTHER STILL ON LOOSE. And so she expected a big lecture on how unsafe it was for her to continue with her internship. But she could tell zoos and leopards weren't what were on her mother's mind.

"What's up?" Kelly couldn't help asking.

"Ed Finnegan, the detective, thinks he may have a lead on Heather out in San Francisco. Some kids think they recognize her from the photos. She might be hanging out at this rock club, doing techie work — and I'm sure she's still dreaming of becoming a big star. Oh honey, maybe we can find her and persuade her to come home, at least to finish junior college, and *then* she can go to California."

From the flush in her mother's cheeks, Kelly could see how thrilled she was by just the idea of getting Heather back, of having her family safe and together again.

"He wants us to fly out there," her mother informed her.

"When?"

"As soon as possible. Tomorrow if we can get reservations. I hate to leave you alone. Especially with that damn cat roaming around."

"Oh, don't worry, they'll have caught it by then. How long can a leopard hide in a small town? I mean, as soon as he goes into the 7-Eleven to buy kitty litter, they're going to nab him."

Her mother smiled. A great thing about her was how much she appreciated Kelly's sense of humor. It was the easiest way to get her out of her worries.

"Okay," her mother said, spooning eggs onto Kelly's plate, "but promise me you won't take any more risks, that you'll get a ride to and from work with Rachel. Et cetera, et cetera . . ."

"Et cetera," Kelly finished for her. "Don't worry about me. If you've got a chance of finding that sister of mine, go for it. I want her back almost as much as you do. I only say *almost* because if she comes back, it means I have to share a bathroom again."

Her mother's response to this was to fake-flick a dishtowel, whiplike, at her.

The truth was, Kelly wasn't crazy about her parents leaving her home alone with everything that was happening. But she couldn't really say this since she didn't want them to *know* everything that was happening. She was kind of caught in her own Catch-22.

\* \* \*

Kelly was amazed to find Sandy in the locker room when she got to work, her arm bound up in a bright white bandage, supported by a sling.

"Sandy! Shouldn't you be — I don't know — in intensive care, or traction, or at least home watching the soaps?"

"Naw. Somehow I talked my mom into letting me come back to work. The thing is, I've got fifty-six stitches and my arm looks pretty darn gruesome underneath this bandage, but I don't really feel that bad otherwise. And, to be honest, I don't really want to sit home alone all day thinking about that leopard, wondering where he is. I'd rather be busy and hanging out with people I know. Even if it does mean being around quite a number of large cats." She nodded in the direction of the cat house.

"Kind of like getting back on the horse that threw you," Kelly suggested.

"Right," Sandy said, her voice soft and frightened. "Only it's a horse that growls — and slashes with its claws."

There were very few visitors at the zoo that morning. The rain and the runaway leopard kept all but the hardy and fearless away. Kelly and Rachel worked with Lonnie Bucks, trimming the trees in all the outdoor cat habitats.

The girls worked on the lower branches and pruned the bushes, while Lonnie got up on a high ladder and clipped the topmost branches. The three of them worked well together, and as they went along, he told them a lot about the cats in his care. There was an extra shading of sadness about him today. He was plain-spoken about it.

"I've lost a good friend," he told them.

It was interesting watching him handle the other cats. Before they could work in a habitat, they had to persuade its occupant to move into the adjacent interior area. He was great at coaxing the cats; it was clear most of them had a lot of affection for him.

Kelly stiffened watching him, though. She was more frightened of the cats than ever. She wished she could be more like Lonnie — at ease with these big felines. Humans had, after all, turned out to be more of a threat to them than they were to humans. And they were undeniably beautiful animals, sinewy and fluid in their movements. So strong, built for speed.

But if she had ever been capable of overcoming her fear of them, now, after the incident with Luther, it was probably hopeless. Now when she looked at them pacing their cages, she just saw them as an assemblage of deadly parts. Muscular legs that could spring them out or up or down from any hiding place, onto their prey. Huge fangs, ready to tear at the flesh of that prey. And — somehow the worst to her — the terrifying claws, always lurking, available to rip a victim to shreds. And always, of course, in these negative fantasies, *she* was the victim, the prey.

"Don't you girls try this," Lonnie was saying, as he rubbed the soft furry forehead of Ranger, the mountain lion, who in return closed his eyes and looked as though he was about to begin purring.

Don't worry, I won't, thought Kelly.

"I've been working with them for years," Lonnie went on. "But even now one of them could revert to its wild self and do me in while I'm in the habitat with it. I take the chance 'cause I just love these boys and girls so much after all our time together."

Put this way, said in this moment, Lonnie's attachment to his feline friends didn't sound so peculiar — at least no more peculiar than other people's attachment to their pets. More and more, Kelly didn't think it was Lonnie who had left Luther's cage door open, although she was in a minority on this. Jon had told her and Rachel something he had heard through his mother, who was on the zoo's board of directors — that the spotlight of suspicion was on Lonnie because management had come to view his attachment to the cats as overprotective, especially when combined with his fairly outspoken views on how unhappy he felt they were in captivity.

Even knowing this, though, Kelly didn't think that — understanding big cats as well as he did, including understanding how dangerous they could be — Lonnie would let a leopard loose on the town. All her intuition told her someone else was behind all these awful events. If she could only figure out a reason someone would do this, she might be able to figure out *who* was doing it.

Maybe it was Dr. Hoffstadter, like Melissa said, even though her story sounded like a twisted fairytale. All the animals out of their cages and Dr. Hoffstadter riding the back of an elephant. There was something particularly creepy about this image, of such a fat man riding high up on an elephant's back.

Why were there these stories floating around? Was it that zoos were such creepy places that they bred creepy gossip? Were weird people attracted to zoo work in the first place? She didn't know what to think, except to begin to wonder why she hadn't taken a summer job Xeroxing at her mother's office.

They were done with their tree trimming by midafternoon and Lonnie told the girls to go on and take a break.

"Why don't we go . . . let's see . . . to the snack bar!" Rachel teased Kelly, knowing there was no other place she would rather be — at least as long as Griffin Black was behind the counter.

He was sitting in the corner when they came in, his chair tilted back, his huge basketball player's feet on the tabletop as he read the newspaper.

"We're sure getting a lot of publicity," he said when he looked up and noticed that they'd come in. "Not exactly the sort the zoo wants, of course."

He was wearing little wire-rimmed glasses, which gave him a kind of intellectual look. In combination with the basketball player look, this was devastatingly attractive, at least to Kelly. Rachel just said, "I hope we can talk him into a couple of free Cokes."

Once she had gotten hers, Rachel told them she was going to sit outside. "I'm going to take a break from today's level of mass hysteria around this place and just finish this nice, quiet little murder mystery."

Kelly wasn't sure if Rachel was telling the truth, that she really needed a break, or if she was just giving them a chance to be alone. At any rate, it looked as though Griffin was going to take advantage of the opportunity. As soon as Rachel had gone out onto the patio, he came out from behind the counter and took the stool next to Kelly's, then spun around on it to face her.

"You know," he said, "the other night when somebody came by and said you and Rachel were in trouble, and I didn't know if you were hurt or all right, I got this terrible clenching feeling here." He tapped the center of his chest. "And . . . well . . . I figured it must mean something."

"Not just that you had heartburn from too many of these hot dogs?" she teased.

"Right," he said, smiling at first, but then his expression grew serious and he put his hands around her waist and leaned in to kiss her. And it was the most delicious kiss she'd ever had — soft, but passionate, too. And it went on for what seemed like forever, so long she started to get lost inside it, to forget where they were and who she was.

And then the real world came crashing through in the form of — of course — Melissa Robinson, bursting in the front door, then screeching to a stop like a cartoon character, putting her hands on her hips and saying, "Oh, my. How gauche of me. I hope I'm not interrupting anything important."

Later, when Kelly had time to think, she came up with several biting, witty responses to this, but in the moment, she just felt exposed and vulnerable and became so flustered that she hopped off her stool and rushed outside, her cheeks burning.

It was only when she was standing on the other side of the door that she could begin to think at all clearly about what had just happened. She replayed the scene in her mind.

She looked up to see Rachel sitting, her book in her lap, staring at Kelly with quite a bit of curiosity, her eyebrows arched in expectation. And so, without explaining a bit of what had just occurred, Kelly told her, "Wait a minute. It's not *me* who should be flustered, it's her. And she *was* interrupting something. Why do I always figure everything out a little too late?"

A bewildered Rachel just shrugged, and said, "Search me."

Kelly said glumly, wondering how much of a fool she had appeared to Griffin, "Oh, well. Story of my life."

# Chapter 10

"Hey! Kelly, Rachel! Wait up."

"Oh-oh," Rachel said, looking over her shoulder. "Quick. Do we have any disguises with us so we can get out of here? We're being stalked by Mr. Excitement."

"Be nice," Kelly said, turning to see Jon approaching them, waving for them to stop on their way out of the zoo. As soon as she'd said it, she couldn't think exactly *why* they should be nice, since Jon wasn't really nice about anything, or to anyone.

"Hey," he said now, panting a little from the exertion of catching up with them. "I was just wondering if you guys'd like to come by my house tonight. Watch some videos, maybe. I could order in some Chinese food. My parents left money. They're up at our lake place so I've got the house to myself. Sometimes I kind of rattle around there on weekends, if you know what I mean."

He was rambling, Kelly thought. Probably nervous about extending the invitation. And what was it about, this sudden, blurted-out invitation? Was he interested in her, or in Rachel maybe? Or was he just lonely at home and wanted company? Was he scared to be home alone with the leopard on the loose? She knew *she* was, although not quite scared enough to make an evening with Jon and his videos and his Chinese food seem like a better alternative.

Still, she tried to be sympathetic.

"I know what you mean about rattling around. My parents are out of town, too, and I get really scared sometimes, hear noises. You know." She meant to stop there, and so she really wasn't sure what she was doing when she heard the words, "Sure, why not? We could come over," slipping past her lips. She looked at Rachel's astonished expression, an expression that said, *Girl, are you crazy?*

"Rachel, what do you say?" she said, and then for emphasis, reached under the jacket Rachel was carrying and pinched her arm.

"Ouch," Rachel said. "I mean, uh, sure. Sounds like fun."

"Okay, then," Jon said. "See you guys about seven?"

When he was out of earshot, Rachel turned to Kelly and said, "Have you lost your mind? A whole night with that geek?"

"But that's the point," Kelly said. "I think he asked us because he's so lonely. He just sounded so desperate under all that rattling on. Maybe his awfulness is just a cover for being shy. I just blew it in there" — she gestured back toward the snack bar — "with Griffin by being totally inept. So how could I turn around and reject this poor guy for being even more totally inept?"

"I think," Rachel said, "that totally inept is as inept as you can be. I don't think there is such a thing as *more* totally inept."

Kelly had to laugh, but then grabbed Rachel before she could get into the car. "So, please. Say you'll come with me. Don't duck out of this. Have mercy on me. I can't spend a social evening alone with Jon."

"Oh, I'll come. But you owe me big time. When the Lippizaner horses come to Springfield again, you have to come with me."

"Argh," Kelly said. Rachel loved this show and had dragged Kelly there once for the most boring night of her life. "Okay. Giant, stupid, boring white dancing horses it is."

Jon was Mr. Host as soon as they walked through the door of his parents' house, which was big, but not a mansion. The furniture looked as though it had been bought all at once in one of those places where the furniture is all grouped into rooms. Everything matched or contrasted and was perfectly dusted with no magazines or bowls of last night's popcorn kernels sitting on a table.

"I already called and ordered the food," Jon said. "Come on into the family room. I picked out a couple of my favorite videos. I thought we could start watching, then eat whenever the food gets here."

"Okay," Kelly said as the three of them settled onto a long, swooping sofa that wound itself around in front of the big-screen TV.

Jon popped a tape in. "Maybe you've already seen this one. *Jungle Prison Camp?*"

"Oh, yeah, it's one of our all-time favorites," Rachel said, being sarcastic, thinking he was, too. But when the video started rolling, it was clear that he wasn't. For the next hour and a half — with a brief intermission when the delivery boy showed up with a bag full of moo shoo pork, fried rice, and Singapore rice noodles — they watched a harrowing pageant of violence. Guys getting their heads sliced off. Falling into pits of quicksand. Walking into a trap where a giant log with spikes poking out of it like a porcupine comes swinging down on chains. Kelly spent most of the time hiding her eyes behind her hands. Rachel was riveted to the screen, but in horror. Jon watched leaning forward from the sofa, cheering on the movie's hero.

"Yes!" he'd say. Or, "excellent work, man!" when something particularly gory happened.

"How can you watch this garbage?" Rachel asked him frankly when the credits were rolling.

"Oh, you get into it after a while. You don't really notice the violence."

"But that's all there *is*," Rachel pointed out.

"You want to see the rest of the house?" he asked.

"Like the torture chamber, maybe?" Rachel said sarcastically.

"Oh, come on," he said, leading the way upstairs, showing them his parents' room, which was like the living room, only with a canopy bed instead of a sofa.

When he opened the door of his room, though, they were in a world separate from the clean and tidy, decorating-magazine rest of the house. The room was painted black, like a dungeon. Hanging on the walls were swords and chains, a decorative axe, a spiked mace. And huge posters of martial arts movie stars. Bruce Lee, Kelly recognized, but none of the others. One attracted her attention immediately. She wondered if Rachel noticed it. The actor was huge, with a steely gaze and raised hands. But it was his upper arm that drew her gaze. On it was a large tattoo of the paw of a jungle cat, its claws outstretched and drawing blood, as if from the man's own flesh.

A little while later, they were saying good night to Jon, who acted as though the evening had been a big social success.

"Hey, that was great. Let's do it again soon!" he said, while Kelly and Rachel tried to think of something to say back, and failed.

When they were in the car and backing out the drive toward the street, Kelly asked Rachel, "Did you see it?"

"See what?"

"The poster."

"Which one? They were all such fascinating-looking guys. Guys you'd love to date because the conversation would be so intellectually stimulating."

"No. There was one in particular. The guy

had this tattoo . . ." She described it in detail.

"Wow," Rachel said and whistled as she drove. By now they were on their way to Kelly's house. "That does seem pretty weirdly coincidental. Do you think it's him, then? Jon. Making all these threats? Letting Luther out of the cage?"

"Well, I was thinking. He *does* know the zoo pretty well from his mother being on the board. He might have known, for instance, where Lonnie hung his keys at night."

"And he hates the job there," Rachel mused. "I think there's a strong possibility he's the one."

"Great," Kelly said, slapping her forehead. "The guy has claws on his wall and I just told him tonight that my parents are out of town!"

# Chapter 11

Rachel left the engine running when she pulled up in front of Kelly's house.

"Rachel," Kelly said, her fear of the leopard and Jon and the unknown all having grown during the drive over, "can you sleep over here tonight?"

Her heart sank when Rachel shook her head. "You know I would. I know you must be jittery with your folks out of town, but I can't. My mom is going to help my aunt early tomorrow — Aunt Esther has a job interview and needs help taking care of her own kids and so my mother needs me to take care of Stephen while she's gone. So I've got to be home tonight."

"Oh. Okay. No problem." Kelly wasn't sure why she felt so frightened. Their house had locks, windows, and doors. It wasn't as though she were camping in a tent in the wilderness.

"I'm being a total baby. Forget it. Just give me a call tomorrow morning. If there's no answer, get worried. Or if something answers with a big meow . . ." It was a lame joke, but she didn't want Rachel worrying about her. She gave what she hoped was a brave little salute as she got out of the car.

She stayed up all the way through David Letterman, then watched part of a movie until she was exhausted enough that she thought she might be able to get to sleep. She tossed and turned and tangled the covers for what seemed like hours.

The house seemed a very different place from when her parents were home, her father snoring, her mother leaving for work, making the "lunch" she would eat in the early morning hours at her job. Without the comforting presence of her parents, the house seemed to take over with its own noises, its own life. Creaking floorboards and rattling shutters. The furnace kicking on, the refrigerator compressor cranking off and then as suddenly starting up again. Noodle's collar tags jingling on the floor as he turned over and stretched in the hallway outside her room. Every noise seemed hugely loud and snapped her back awake out of whatever light sleep she'd been able to slide into.

I'm being ridiculous, she thought. I'm just scaring myself. I'm going to put all this nonsense out of my mind and. . . . As she was finishing this sensible thought, she happened to turn over and open her eyes just in time to see a huge, terrifying shadow creeping across the hall, what appeared to be a giant cat slowly creeping across the top of her dresser, raising then stretching out its paw, forcing out a full set of sharp claws. She lay riveted to this sight, watching the shadow cat drop to the floor. She shot out of bed, shaking, and rushed over to turn on the light switch.

"Meow?" said her cat, Marilyn Monroe, as if to say, What's the problem? She then hopped back up onto the dresser.

Kelly switched off the overhead light again and saw how the streetlamp played tricks and turned a small house cat into a stalking leopard. She collapsed against the wall, trembling and laughing in relief, then swooping up her little tabby with one hand, holding her in midair.

But then, when Marilyn, disoriented and a little frightened at being snatched up off the floor like this, defended herself by swiping a paw through the air, claws extended, fangs showing as she hissed, Kelly once again saw the face of Luther coming at her. She let the cat go and stood shaking in the middle of her room, irrational tears sliding down her cheeks.

The next morning Kelly flipped on the TV on the kitchen counter as she poured some granola into a bowl. She almost overflowed the bowl when she immediately became absorbed by what she saw on the set.

The police had Luther cornered at some farm outside town, and a TV camera crew had gotten there in time to catch the action around an abandoned barn where the black leopard had apparently hidden himself. With nets and guns, tactical police and zoo security officers had the big cat cornered. But Luther was too fast, too wily for them. It was so fast it was nearly a blur as the cat shot between two of its uniformed, would-be captors, out into the fields of the farm, then into a stand of woods in the distance.

Several guns went off, but none made contact with the fleeing cat.

"Officials here don't want to kill the leopard if they can at all avoid it," said the newscaster. "Like most of the animals at the zoo, the black leopard is an endangered species. Although its range is still nearly as large as it once was, there are fewer leopards within the range, and so fewer exist in the wild, and animal rights activists are leery of killing one of the few such big cats living in captivity. And so the guns you see being fired are armed with only tranquilizer darts to subdue the animal enough to bring it back to the Creighton Gardens Zoo."

Kelly watched, riveted, as the security and police officials got into their cars and four-wheel drive vehicles and headed out after Luther. Even though this was happening outside of town and she was seeing it through the safe filter of the television, she still felt a chill pass through her, watching the big cat move so swiftly. She could still see it in her mind's eye racing toward her.

"Oh, no!" she said aloud to the empty kitchen. "He got away. But where to?"

A little later, Kelly and Rachel pushed open the door to the women employees' locker room and entered to find themselves in the middle of a scene. Sandy was there. Pam Perkins, too, which was unusual. She was sitting next to Melissa, comforting the girl as she wept.

"Why me? Why *my* locker?" Melissa was saying, her hand covering her eyes as she sobbed.

"What's happening?" Rachel said.

Melissa kept sobbing while Pam explained, "She came in early this morning to find this . . ." Pam gestured toward the door of Melissa's locker. When Kelly and Rachel moved closer they could see what Pam was referring to — a nasty set of gouges in the paint, long scratches in the metal, five of them that seemed to have been made with the claws of a large cat.

"Oh, no," Kelly breathed.

"Luther is back?" Rachel guessed.

"If he is, no one has seen him," Pam said. "The last report was when they found him at that farm earlier this morning. He can't have been in two places at once, so we suspect this was made by one of the other cats here — sometime during the night."

"But the other cats are locked in their cages and habitats," Kelly said, not getting what Pam was saying.

"Apparently at least one of them was out during the night," Pam clarified. "Apparently someone *let* it out."

"Isn't there *any* security around this place?" Kelly wondered aloud.

"Well," Pam said, a defensive tone creeping into her voice, "we hadn't had any trouble like this before. And then when Luther escaped, Lonnie of course stopped hanging his keys out in the open on that hook."

"But if the keys weren't there," Rachel said, "then how could someone have opened the cage? Are there other keys?"

"Well, of course, other zoo personnel have access to the cages and habitats," Pam said. "Security. Management. Veterinary services."

"So lots of people could have got hold of those keys," Rachel said.

"Well, yes," Pam admitted. "If they knew where to look."

"So," Kelly said, "whoever is doing these things has some connection to the zoo, knows it pretty well."

Pam looked up at Kelly, a little surprised, it seemed. "Boy, you girls are sharp detectives."

"Well, we'd like to find whoever's doing this," Kelly said. "The threats have all been against us interns. You want to save the zoo, but we have an even more special interest. We'd like to save ourselves."

# Chapter 12

"I'm having a 'Chase the Blues' party," Melissa told everyone that afternoon when the interns had gathered in the snack bar before heading home. "I refuse to be intimidated by all these weird goings-on. Let's wipe away the gloom and party hearty, what do you all say?" She shook her hair back off her shoulders, first to one side, then the other.

"Sounds like a good idea to me," Griffin said. "We're all letting this cat stuff get us down when we should be doing something to shake it off."

"I'd like to see if I could dance with this arm in a sling," Sandy said, laughing at herself.

"I never turn down a party invitation," Jon said.

"I'll bet he doesn't," Rachel said under her breath to Kelly. "He probably gets about one a year."

"When though?" said Sandy.

"What about tomorrow night?" Melissa said. "Friday."

Everyone said they could come.

"Great. I'll invite a few other kids I know and get my mother to lay in some goodies. Nachos. Dips. Soda."

"Beer," Jon said.

"In your dreams," Melissa said, giving him a broad wink. "You'll have to sneak that in yourself."

Kelly had begun to notice that both Melissa and Jon talked a good game about being wild and having killer social lives, but she suspected they were both actually lonely and unpopular people trying to cover this up. She was trying to be charitable in her thoughts toward both of them, to make up for not liking them. This wasn't easy. Just as Kelly was filling herself with resolve to be kind to and open-minded about the two of them, Melissa was saying, "Of course, perhaps I should ask *ma mere* to order some caviar . . ." while Jon was doing something with a zit on his neck that should have waited until he got home.

Later, when Rachel and Kelly were at Kelly's house fixing themselves a peanut butter and banana sandwich dinner, a pensive look crossed Rachel's face. At first Kelly just thought she was trying to get her mouth unstuck from the peanut butter, but when she was finally able to speak, what she said was pretty shocking.

"I don't want to freak you out, Kel, but I think we ought to go back to the zoo tonight. Late."

"What? Why?" Kelly shouted. "And anyway — whatever your reason — absolutely not, no way!"

"Look. Something's going on there, and it's not happening while the place is open and everyone's around. If we're ever going to figure out what's going on, I think we're going to have to hang out in the darkest shadows and see what we see. It scares me, too, but I'm willing to try."

Kelly swallowed a mouthful of milk as if it were a stone. She thought the idea over. "Well, since I jumped at Marilyn Monroe's shadow, I guess I'm clearly afraid to be in this house at night. I don't want to be alone here. I suppose it wouldn't be much worse at the zoo. At least we'd be together. But how are we going to get in?"

Rachel pulled a serious-looking key out of

her pocket. "Sometimes the zoo's loose security works against you, sometimes it works in your favor," she said.

They planned to leave around midnight. Until then, they killed time microwaving popcorn, playing with Noodle and Marilyn Monroe, and flipping through the late-night world of cable. Kelly's parents called in around ten and she reassured them that everything was fine.

"Yes, I'm all locked in. Rachel's here with me. No, they haven't caught the leopard yet, but you know they will any minute now."

"The parent massage," Rachel said when Kelly had hung up.

"Well, what am I going to say? Oh, by the way, Rachel and I are just hanging out here until we leave the house around midnight to go over and break into the zoo so we can do some amateur spying. *Right.*"

Around eleven-thirty, they started getting dressed. Rachel borrowed clothes from Kelly so they could both wear black tights and black turtlenecks. They put on running shoes so they could be fast if they needed to. They each brought a flashlight.

When they got to the zoo, Rachel parked on the street outside, then they walked up the long gravel drive with the narrow beams of their flashlights guiding them. From a distance, they could hear the cries of some of the exotic birds. Loons. Macaws.

Kelly shivered.

"Cold?" Rachel said.

"No. Scared."

"Me, too," Rachel said. "But we can't afford to be scared. We've got a mission."

"I'm sorry. I said I'd come along with you, but I can't instantly sprout nerves of steel, too. I'm just a beginner at being brave, and you'll just have to accept me that way."

Rachel grabbed Kelly's hand. "Okay. You just do the best you can."

When they got to the side gate, Rachel slid in her key. She had to fiddle with it a while, but eventually it turned and they slipped inside, holding the huge iron gate behind them as it closed. They didn't want it clanking shut, exposing their presence.

"Who's in here at night?" Rachel wondered aloud.

"Well, the security guys, I'd think," Kelly said. "Although most of them are probably out combing the town for Luther now. We might find nobody home here."

The old-fashioned streetlamps that lined the paths of the zoo had been turned off, and it was eerie walking past all the animal habitats in pitch darkness. They only knew where they were by the screech of the bird inside, or the trumpeting of the elephant, or the splashing of the polar bears in their pond. Each time they passed a habitat, they roused the animals within, who smelled their human strangeness. Night was clearly the time when the zoo reverted to being a place reserved for animals. Humans were invasive in these private hours and all the species were letting them know they were noticed and not particularly welcome.

"Nothing unusual so far," Rachel said when they'd made a circuit of half the zoo.

"*We're* probably the only thing unusual in here. Notice how we're riling the poor things. Maybe we ought to just leave."

"No way. Something weird's going on in this zoo and I'm not going to rest until I've found it," Rachel said.

They proceeded in darkness for another short distance. Then, as they rounded the corner of the bird house, heading toward the primate house, they were suddenly aware of light that wasn't coming from their flashlights. The central large primate habitat was lit from within and cast a soft skirt of yellow onto the walkway. When they got a little closer, they could hear music. Someone was playing "Greensleeves" on a reed instrument, a flute or recorder.

Kelly gave Rachel a question mark look. "What? Who?" she said.

Rachel pressed a finger to her lips. "Don't know. Put your mask on, though, in case we run into someone," she whispered.

They had brought along rubber Halloween masks from Kelly's basement. The Terminator and Frankenstein. They pulled the elastic bands around the backs of their heads and lined up the eyeholes of the masks so they could see out without being identifiable.

"Move slowly," Rachel cautioned. "I want to see who or what is having a concert in that gorilla habitat."

They crept up to the edge of the large primate habitat — a sort of playpen for the gorillas and orangutans — then Kelly stuck her head slowly around to peer in. What she saw was so strange she actually blinked and took a second look to make sure she wasn't fantasizing it.

There, in the midst of a collection of rapt and silent primates — sitting on tree branches or hanging from them, perched on rock shelves as though they were nearly human concertgoers — sat Dr. Hoffstadter, straight-backed on one of the folding chairs from the gazebo, sheet music propped on a metal stand in front of him, wearing a baggy old tuxedo, his eyes closed dreamily as he played a private flute concert for the monkeys.

Kelly backed away to let Rachel by so she could get a look at this unbelievable sight. Then they both flattened themselves against the bricks to the side of the habitat.

"I feel like Alice when she dropped down the rabbit hole into Wonderland," Rachel whispered into Kelly's ear.

Kelly just nodded, shocked by what she had seen. After a moment, she thought to ask, "Did he see us?"

Rachel shook her head. "I don't think so. He's pretty wrapped up in his playing."

But even as she was speaking, the music stopped abruptly, in the middle of a note. The girls, pressing themselves as flat as they could against the building, held their breath. But it was no use. The gorillas were jumping up and down, the orangutans swinging from branch to branch, all of them grunting and cooing and squealing.

"We've been smelled out," Rachel said.

"Who's there?" Dr. Hoffstadter shouted into the darkness that hid the girls away from him. "I know you're out there. If you don't come forward and identify yourself, I'll be forced to consider you a security risk to the zoo and use this weapon."

"Weapon?" the girls mouthed to each other simultaneously.

"Maybe he's bluffing," Kelly said.

"Probably," Rachel agreed. "But just in case he isn't, I say we make a break for the gate."

Kelly nodded and they both slipped away from the wall and began loping off, down the walkway, toward the side gate.

"Halt, I said! I am in charge of these premises and will take all necessary measures to protect my zoo," they heard Dr. Hoffstadter shout, followed almost immediately by what at first Kelly took to be the air raid test siren on the old town water tower.

Rachel brought her into reality. "He's activated the zoo's alarm system!" she shouted. "We'd better get out of here!"

By now almost every animal in the zoo was awake and screeching or growling or baying or cawing. The air was alive with noise. The two of them took off as fast as their feet could carry them.

"Can you run any faster?" Kelly shouted. She knew her friend wasn't a runner, wasn't in the kind of condition she herself was.

"No," Rachel said. "This is the best I can do. Go on ahead if you can."

"No way," Kelly said, matching her strides to her friend's slower pace. "We're in this together, through thick and thin."

"Is this the thick," Rachel panted, "or the thin?"

Before she could get the weak joke out, they heard the heavy footfalls of a number of security guards. Kelly looked over her shoulder and saw four burly men in uniforms bearing down on them.

"Come on!" she shouted at Rachel, who was starting to fall behind. "There's the gate. We can make it if you give it one last burst."

"I can't," Rachel moaned. "I'm running out of steam. You go on ahead. Save your own skin."

Kelly didn't bother to dignify this with an answer; she just took Rachel's arm and pulled her the rest of the way to the gate. When they got there, she pulled it open, pushed Rachel through, then slipped out herself, and dragged Rachel by the hand down the gravel drive to the car, which — miraculously — started with the first turn of the key, and they were off.

Neither of them said anything until they'd gone about a mile and Rachel pulled onto a small residential street and parked under a tree.

"Oh, Kel, I'm sorry I got you into that," she said as they both realized they still had their masks on, and pulled them off, laughing — almost hysterically.

"Forget it," Kelly said. "We're okay now. And we did see something incredible. I still can't believe it."

"Yeah," Rachel muttered. "But does it have *anything* to do with the plot against the interns?"

"What do you mean? The guy was playing his flute for the gorillas. He was wearing a tuxedo. He's a nut," Kelly said.

"So? He's peculiar. That doesn't mean he's dangerous. Unless he is so mondo-peculiar about the zoo that he doesn't want interlopers like the interns coming into it and he's trying to scare us away," Rachel said. "On the other hand, he might just be a guy who enjoys playing for an audience of appreciative primates. The more we hang around Creeping Gardens, the more the weird begins to seem almost normal."

# Chapter 13

Almost the strangest thing about Kelly and Rachel's nocturnal visit to the zoo was that there was no mention of unknown intruders in the paper Kelly picked up off her front porch the next morning. And nothing was said about it when she got to work.

She even saw Dr. Hoffstadter — out of his tuxedo and back in one of his bunchy old brown suits — as he was supervising the arrival at the zoo of two new bear cubs.

"He seems back to normal," Rachel said, then added, "Well, as normal as Dr. Hoffstadter gets, that is."

"Why isn't the place in an uproar, though, I wonder?" Kelly said. "Security guards have to chase after disguised intruders. You would think there'd at least be a meeting to warn employees."

"Hoffstadter probably doesn't want everyone knowing about his nighttime activities."

Kelly wanted to drop by the snack bar and tell Griffin what they'd done and seen, but she was too embarrassed about having run out of the snack bar yesterday. She was hoping he would come to Melissa's party that night and she would have a chance to be a little cooler around him.

As it turned out, the "few other kids" Melissa was going to invite to her party turned out to be about fifty of them, most of whom Kelly didn't know. By the time she and Rachel arrived, the party was in high gear. Melissa's parents had hired a disk jockey and so the music was loud and seamless, the back deck of the house transformed into a throbbing dance floor.

On the lawn behind the house, a buffet table was set with a full array of food in a Mexican theme. Tacos and guacamole. Nachos. Rice and beans. The bar featured all kinds of soda and sparkling water and a large punch bowl, which Kelly heard was filled only with fruit juice when Mr. and Mrs. Robinson had set it out, but was now about half alcohol, thanks to the sneaky contributions of various guests. She saw some kids near the edges of the yard with cans of beer.

Kelly could see from their style (lots of pierced noses and eyebrows, magenta hair, big boots) that Melissa's friends were a wilder crowd than the one she and Rachel hung around with. Of course, who knows how close Melissa was to any of these party guests? She could easily imagine her inviting a houseful of kids she barely knew, just because they were ultra-hip looking and she wanted to seem ultra-hip.

"Quite a place," Rachel said, coming over to where Kelly was standing at the edge of the deck, having a Coke.

"Yeah. I wonder what it would be like to live in this sort of luxury."

"Want to snoop around a little?" Rachel said, knowing full well that Kelly — terrible snoop that she was — would find the invitation irresistible.

The two of them moved slowly across the deck, through the sliding glass doors, and into the house.

Upstairs they gave themselves a tour of Melissa's room, which had a queen-size waterbed, its own stereo set, and computer area. Then they tried a few more doors along the hallway and wound up in Mr. and Mrs. Robinson's master suite, which was sort of a combination bedroom/health spa with an array of exercise equipment. By one side of the giant canopied bed there was an oil painting on hinges, like a little door. It was open, revealing that behind it was a small safe with an impressive-looking dial lock.

"Why would someone have a safe in their bedroom?" Rachel wondered aloud.

"To protect their valuables, of course," Kelly said, going over for a closer look, twirling the dial a few times back and forth. "Our families don't have a safe because we don't have to worry about burglars taking our plastic dinnerware and jewelry from Kmart. It looks as though these people really have money."

"Yeah," Rachel said in her "thinking deep" tone of voice. "Mr. Robinson's doing pretty well for an accountant, don't you think?"

"What are you saying?"

"Just that I thought accountants were kind of middle-income types."

"Maybe he's something bigger than that. An investment consultant or something. Maybe he has a ton of other clients," Kelly said.

"No, I distinctly remember Melissa saying the zoo books took up all his time."

"So? What are you getting at?" Kelly asked. "I know you're getting at something."

"Nothing firm," Rachel said, mulling. "Just an idea. I'll let you know when I've worked it out a little more."

By the time the girls got back downstairs, the party had gotten even bigger and rowdier. Kelly didn't care how many kids arrived, though. There was really only one guest she was interested in. She scanned the room and, happily, there he was. Griffin had arrived.

He looked terrific. She had gotten used to seeing him in his snack shop "uniform" of white T-shirt and jeans, with a kitchen apron over the whole thing and a Creighton Gardens baseball cap turned around on his head. She realized she had never seen him dressed up. Tonight, though, he was wearing pleated khakis and a dark denim shirt with a wild Hawaiian print tie. White leather basketball shoes. When she approached him to talk, she couldn't help noticing he was also wearing a spicy aftershave that tickled the inside of her nose.

"Hey, you look great," she told him.

"Not bad yourself," he said, and she was glad she'd gone to a little trouble, putting together what she thought was a pretty cool outfit — long, baggy white shorts, a navy shirt and a forest green vest. This was the kind of look she liked best on herself — put-together, but not as though she had been trying too hard to put it together.

"Hey, I know I acted like a goon the other

day," she said. "Running out of the snack bar like that."

"It's okay. As it turns out, I have a weakness for goony girls. In fact . . ."

But he didn't have a chance to finish as their hostess materialized on the scene almost instantly.

"Griffin," Melissa said in a tone that was nearly a squeal. "I was beginning to think you weren't going to show up."

"Oh," he said, smiling slyly, "I wasn't about to miss tonight." Kelly suspected he meant because of her, but Melissa managed to interpret this as referring to herself, that Griffin was here on account of her.

"You are so sweet," she said. "And so cute. Getting all dressed up like that. Come with me, will you, for a little bit? There are some friends of mine I'd like you to meet."

And with that she dragged him off across the dance floor.

Kelly expected him back right away, but when half an hour turned to an hour, her heart began to sink. She didn't want to go looking for him; that would be too obvious. And what would she find — just that he was off in some corner of the party having fun with Melissa and some friends of hers? Or worse, that the two of them were off someplace further removed from the party, having a more private sort of fun?

Her thoughts had reached a pretty gloomy point when she looked up and saw him coming across the backyard toward her. By this time, she was sitting out on the lawn, thinking about leaving the party.

"Sorry," he said, sitting down next to her.

"It's okay," she said.

"I'm too polite sometimes," he said, wrapping her hand in his. "I have trouble getting out of stupid situations."

"I suspect Melissa cooked up this whole party idea just to get you into a compromising situation."

"I think Melissa is a person who has gotten everything she's wanted all her life and now she wants me and can't understand why she can't have me," Griffin said.

"Why not? She's great looking, not to mention fabulously wealthy. Why not go for it?"

"Well, I guess because I've got somebody else in mind."

And then they were kissing and she forgot for the moment about telling him the story about Dr. Hoffstadter, forgot even to care if someone looked over and saw. Particularly not if that person was Melissa.

# Chapter 14

Kelly was awakened Saturday around noon by the phone ringing.

"Yeah?" she said groggily. "I mean, hello?"

"Honey, are you all right?" She recognized her mother's voice. There was what sounded like water running in the background.

"I'm fine. This was my first day off work. I guess I just slept in like a total slob." She stretched and sat up in bed. "Where's Dad?"

"He's in the shower. We're here in our hotel room."

"How's it going? Are you making any progress?"

"Oh, I don't know," her mother said, her voice filled with weariness. "At first we thought we were very close, but the girl Finnegan had found wasn't Heather. She just looked remarkably like her and also wanted to be an actress. When that lead turned cold, we were back where we started from. But since we're already out here, your father and I think we ought to stay a couple more days to check out a few possibilities. How are you holding up without us? Do you need us to come home now, because if you do . . ."

"Oh no, that's okay. If you think you might be able to do some good out there, stay. I'm fine." This wasn't quite true. Kelly would much rather her parents come back today as they had said they would. Ordinarily, she would have welcomed a chance for a few more days of ordering pizza every night for dinner and staying up as late as she wanted with no one yelling for her to get in bed, or get off the phone. But with all the weird things that had been happening lately, and with the leopard still on the loose, what she most wanted to do was be seven years old again, with Mommy and Daddy there to take care of her.

But she didn't want to let *them* know that. Actually, at this point, there was just too much she couldn't let them know. She and Rachel were determined to find out what was going on at the zoo, and if she told her parents, they'd have her out of the internship and into that Xerox-copying position her mom had lined up at her office. No, if she was going to follow through on this, she would have to keep the whole thing from them for a little while longer.

Plus, she was hoping against hope that, while they were in California, they *would* find Heather. Although Kelly had a lot of confidence in her sister's smartness and toughness and perseverance, she was nonetheless beginning to worry now that several months had gone by and Heather had not gotten in touch with their parents, with her, or with her best friend, Lisa. Maybe something bad *had* happened to Heather.

"Just do whatever you need to," Kelly told her mother. "I'm fine here. Rachel's staying with me anyway," she lied. Her mother always said Rachel was a forty-year-old woman in a teenager's body.

"Probably a stricter parent than I am," she said to Kelly now. "Lets you eat fewer sweets."

When Kelly had hung up, she went downstairs and pulled a giant bottle of Coke out of the fridge, then gulped from it standing in front of the kitchen window.

If she was going to get a run in, she'd better go soon. She got dressed in shorts and a tank top, pulled on her running socks and shoes, found a tape with a heavy beat (old Bruce Springsteen) for her Walkman, and headed out.

She ran to the end of her street — Willow — which was where the town gave way to the countryside surrounding it. For about half a mile, the narrow road led past the Hagstroms' farmland, then wound into a wooded area that was nearly dark as night from the storm clouds that covered the sky like a thick, dark gray putty.

Maybe I ought to just head back, in case it starts to pour, she thought. But it felt so great to be out, running free after this week of so much fear and tension. She decided to go just half a mile further, then take a shortcut back.

As she ran, it occurred to her that she hadn't seen a car or bike or another person on foot since she had gotten out of town. Of course, with the oncoming storm, who but a running nut like herself would be out now? Plus, many people in town were staying inside their houses these days, with Luther still roaming around somewhere. Even on Main Street, there was a ghost town atmosphere to the normally lively downtown district of Danube. Nowadays, people got their groceries, gassed up their cars, picked up a couple of videos, and went straight home. Everyone was afraid.

About the only crowd Kelly had seen lately was at the town meeting a few nights before. Almost everyone had attended. In the safe confines of the high school auditorium people didn't seem frightened so much as angry. Angry at Dr. Hoffstadter, who tried to explain the zoo's security systems and practically got booed off the stage. They were also angry at the police, who still had not been able to come up with a trace of a dangerous black leopard.

There had been clues. The mauled carcasses of two sheep had been found by Gill Keanen on his pastureland the day before yesterday, so it looked as though Luther was able to elude his captors and find food to live on. This made everyone even angrier. The auditorium erupted after Gill revealed his story. Kelly suspected the anger was a cover for fear. No one knew what to do about the leopard, and individually each person was cold at heart with fear, but together they could afford to be angry and were looking for someone to be angry *at*.

Kelly was determined not to let this kind of fear overwhelm her. She refused to stop her life because some big cat was out there. Even though she was afraid of Luther, she had an advantage in a way — unlike most of the people at the meeting, she had faced the cat down and lived to tell about it.

Still, today, all alone on her run, she felt a chill passing through her that had nothing to do with the weather, which was warm and muggy. The free and easy feeling she usually had while running was disappearing, replaced by an eeriness inside her.

Finally she found the shortcut — a narrow blacktop road that circled back to her side of town — and took it. Although this route had the advantage of being shorter, it would keep her in dense woods the whole way. At this moment they were so dark she felt it was midnight.

She picked up her pace, and turned up the volume knob on her Walkman, letting Bruce Springsteen fill in the chasm of silence she was running through. Usually the music absorbed her, but right now she was too nervous to get caught up in it. Her eyes darted left and right, and so she saw him right away, from quite a ways off. To the side, in among the thicket of birch trees to one side of the road. A tall, thin man and a large, dark animal he appeared to be training, or maybe just playing with.

Then, as she was staring at him, a most amazing thing happened — he waved to her, first a wave of greeting, then with a beckoning motion of his hand. *Come over*, it said.

Yeah, right, buddy, she thought. Like I'm about to go over to visit some strange man in the middle of the woods on a dark, deserted stretch of road. Maybe I'll take some candy from you while I'm at it.

But he kept waving and as she got closer he did look slightly more familiar. Tall, thin, slightly stoop-shouldered. And the animal he was playing with — roughhousing it appeared — was large and dark. She couldn't tell any more than that. Both were too far off and unless she left the road, she wouldn't be able to get a better look at either of them. And she was definitely not getting off the road.

It wasn't until a mile or so on, when she was almost back to the edge of town, that it hit her — the man had been Lonnie Bucks! She couldn't be absolutely sure on account of the distance and the slouchy hat he'd been wearing, but she still . . .

Which meant the large, dark animal he was training and playing with out there in that isolated wooded area was . . .

No. It couldn't be.

# Chapter 15

The first thing she did when she got back was call Rachel, but she got only an answering machine. She was about to jump out of her skin. She had to talk with someone about what she had just seen — someone who would understand. She thought for a moment, weighed the pros and cons, and then started dialing Griffin's number. She was pretty sure he would understand that she was calling because she needed to talk. And, if he thought she was just flirting . . . well, she'd just have to take that chance.

Luckily, he was home. His father called him in from outside and he picked up the receiver out of breath.

"Listen, something just happened . . ." she started in, not knowing quite where to begin.

"Hey, wait. First, are you okay?" he sounded truly concerned.

"I'm fine. It's just something peculiar I saw when I was out for my run just now. Something I need to talk with you about. Did I get you at a bad time?"

"Sort of," he said, and laughed. "My dad's waiting in the driveway. Gunning the motor, can you hear? I'm supposed to go over to Crosby Corners with him to take in our lawn mower, which died a hideous death today. If this can wait a couple of hours, why don't I stop by when I get free of the parental clutches and you can tell me every detail of whatever it was you saw — okay?"

"Okay," she said. But she wished he could have come right over.

She sat staring at the phone, trying to think of someone else she could talk with, but there wasn't anyone. And then suddenly it rang, as if on cue. She picked up.

"Kelly?"

When she heard the male voice, for a second she thought it was Griffin calling back to say he'd gotten out of the lawn mower trip. But almost immediately she recognized the nasal quality of the voice.

"Hi, Jon," she said, trying to be polite, while at the same time not letting the slightest hint of interest into her voice. Because she just *knew* he was going to ask her out.

"I . . . uh . . . was wondering if you were busy tonight," he said nervously. "Because there's this new martial arts flick over . . ."

"Hey, Jon, I'd love to, really. But the thing is, I'm doing something tonight."

"What?"

"What do you mean 'what'? I'm seeing somebody else is what."

"Oh. Who?"

"Well," Kelly said, laughing a little purely out of tension, thinking what nerve he had to be prying like this, but to be polite she said, "Griffin, actually. He's coming over in just a little while, too," she lied, "so I really have to get off the line. But I'll see you at work, hey?"

Before he could worm his way back into some kind of conversation, she hung up the receiver. So he had probably been interested in her when he invited her and Rachel over to watch that gruesome video. She hadn't really picked up on his interest. Probably because she didn't want it.

But her deeper fear was that his interest in her wasn't just a typical crush, but something weirder, creepier, sicker, that involved cats and claws. She shuddered.

\* \* \*

Rachel never called back, and by the time Griffin came over, it was almost dinnertime. He looked as though he had taken her seriously and gotten there as soon as he could, not bothering to change clothes. His khakis were covered with grass stains, and his black T-shirt had a V-shaped sweat stain just beneath the collar.

"Thanks for coming," she said. "For humoring me."

"No problem."

"Hey, are you hungry?"

"Like a wolf."

"What about I fix us something to eat while I tell you what happened? Then if you think I'm crazy, at least you'll think I'm a crazy person who can cook."

Having been on the all-pizza diet for the past couple of days, Kelly knew there wasn't much in the refrigerator to fix a real dinner out of. She wound up making scrambled eggs with cheese in them, and toast with jam.

"Crank up that toaster, and don't put that bread back in the refrigerator," he said, when he saw what she was doing. "I can eat a *lot* of toast."

"How much?"

"Maybe half of that loaf you've got there."
He shrugged. "Something to do with basketball, I guess. The other guys are like this, too.
Maybe we all have hollow legs or something.
Legs that need to be filled with toast!"

She was discovering that he had a distinctly
silly side, which was a relief. Most guys she
met didn't. They were either serious, or made
obvious, clunky jokes. She had been hoping to
eventually meet someone who was like her
— someone who sort of just slid around between serious and silly. Now it looked as
though she had met someone just like this.

He helped her fix their little dinner.

She set their plates of eggs and tomato
slices down on the kitchen table and poured
some orange juice. She put two more slices
of bread into the toaster before they sat down.
"Reinforcements," she told him.

When they'd started eating, he said, "Okay,
now tell me your peculiar story."

And so she did.

"Are you sure it was him?" he asked when
she was finished.

"Pretty sure," she said. "Not positive."

"But if it was, then why would he have called
you over like that? Wouldn't he want to hide
the fact that he had the leopard with him?"

"None of it makes any sense."

"We could check it out. Get his address from the phone book and take a little drive over there. Go by his house and see what's up."

"Good idea," Kelly said, relieved to be doing *something*.

They found the address. It was on a street in a run-down part of town. Dusk had fallen by the time they drove slowly down Lonnie's block. The house was an old, two-story frame box, set back from the street at the end of a deep front yard. There was a picture window in the living room and, with a lamp glowing dimly inside, they could see someone moving about the room, walking from one side to the other, then sitting down in a chair. They could also see a lower, darker shape pacing back and forth across the room, then disappearing from view. And then the human figure stood up and came closer to the window.

"We'd better move on," Griffin said, putting the car in gear and pulling slowly down the street. "We don't want him to spot us here."

"So?" Kelly said when they had turned the corner and pulled over to the curb. "What do you think?"

"I don't know. We were too far away to tell. And the only way we could get up any closer would be on foot, which I'm not quite brave or dumb enough to attempt. If that *is* Luther he's got in there with him, and he let him loose, we could be two leopard snacks in a matter of seconds."

"Right," she said, nodding and thinking the situation over. "But a leopard in his *living room*?"

"On the other hand, it might be another animal. We can't really go to the police and ask them to break in on Lonnie just because of these vague suspicions we have. If nothing's going on, he'll just get freaked out again."

She nodded.

"Let's sleep on it, think of some way we can drop by and pay him a visit without putting ourselves in mortal danger."

She nodded again.

"You just keep nodding at everything I say," he said. "You're being very agreeable tonight."

She couldn't help smiling.

"Would you agree with me no matter what I said?"

"Maybe," she said, smiling some more.

"Let me try," he said, then pretended to be thinking deeply of something she might agree with. "Okay. What about this statement: I think you should kiss me."

And once again, Kelly nodded and smiled,

until she couldn't smile anymore because her lips were covered by his.

It was quite a bit later when Griffin dropped her off at home. He got out of the car and walked her around to the side door, where they started kissing again, for quite a while.

"Maybe I should come in," he said. "Keep you safe tonight."

"Actually, I think that might be even more dangerous than tigers and leopards, only in a different way," she said, and smiled as she pushed him off, down the driveway. She stood and watched as he loped across the lawn toward his car. When he got there, he didn't get in, just stood staring inside.

"Kelly, I think you'd better come down here."

She half ran, half didn't want to see whatever it was he was about to show her. When she got to the edge of the lawn, on the other side of the car from him, she looked inside and saw what he'd just seen by the dim interior light. The front seats — the seats still warm from their body heat — had been viciously slashed. The fabric was split with the stuffing pushing out. At first it looked like random cuts, but when she was able to look more closely, Kelly could see that the marks were grouped in fives. These tears had been made by a claw — the same claw, it appeared, that had scratched Melissa's locker.

She ran to the other side of the car and clung to him, then looked around for a cat on the loose, but didn't see any. They both stood very still to listen for the low growling they had come to be in terror of.

"There's nothing out here," he said, pulling her tighter to him. "Someone's trying to scare us."

"You don't think it's the leopard?"

"Leopards aren't trying to make a point. Whoever did this was. They wanted to mark the places where we'd just been, to make the point that it's us they're after. That's not the thinking of a leopard. To a leopard we are all just dinner. Well," he said, trying to smile, "I might be dinner, but you're smaller. You might just be lunch."

If they kept trying to kid around about the leopard, Kelly found it made them less afraid of what was going on.

"But if it wasn't Luther, if it was a person, then how did they make the marks?" she asked.

"Don't know," he said, shaking his head, touching the ripped upholstery with the tips of his fingers, as if it might burn him. "But we're going to find out. Now go inside and lock up good. Try to get some sleep. I'll call first thing in the morning. And if anything odd happens — anything at all — call me tonight. I'll keep the cordless by my pillow."

# Chapter 16

The first thing she did when she got inside was check the answering machine, but there were no blinks; Rachel still hadn't called back. Odd, she thought, but then everything was odd these days.

With no one around to protect her, Kelly did the best she could on her own. She checked all the doors to be sure they were locked. Then she shut and locked all the windows on the first floor and went upstairs to her room. She put her fan in the window and turned it on high to drown out any creaking noises, any dog or cat thumping — anything that might keep her up or wake her up.

She was almost asleep when her eyelids snapped open with sudden realization — the basement door! They hardly ever used it and so she had completely forgotten to include it in her sequence of checks around the house. She got up, pulled on her jeans and crept downstairs.

Theirs was an old house — nearly a hundred years old — and the basement had never been modernized, so it was a crumbling space with old beams and dusty brick walls and a large charred patch in the ceiling where there had once been a furnace fire. It was Kelly's least favorite place in the house.

She moved quickly and deliberately once she was down there. She didn't want to have to spend any more time in the basement than she had to. With relief, she saw that the door, at the back of a small room formerly used for storing coal, was closed. She gave it a tug and found it locked.

There, she thought. That's that. Now I can go to sleep in peace. But, as she was walking back through the long main room of the basement, an area that was usually dank and musty, she felt a fresh nighttime breeze. At first it was pleasurable. She was able to enjoy the airy sensation for a brief moment before the thought came crashing into her consciousness that breezes have to come from somewhere — but in a room that was always closed?

She searched along all the walls and finally

found the source. Off to the side, high up almost to the ceiling was an old casement window, and it was cranked open. She stood on a trunk and twisted the handle until it was closed again and then did a quick scan of the rest of the basement. Nothing seemed out of place, nothing looked to be missing. Her father had probably opened the window sometime when he was working down there and just forgot to shut it. That was it. She tried to calm herself down. There was doubtless some perfectly boring and reasonable explanation for this window being open. The only thing was, it had never been open before.

She thought a moment, then went upstairs, grabbed a flashlight in the kitchen, and went outside. She looked around carefully, but saw nothing. She walked around to the side of the house that the window opened onto and ran the beam from the light across the ground, and there it was in the dirt in front of the window — what she had been dreading. The mark of a large cat, five claw marks etched into the earth. The same sort of mark that had been slashed through Griffin's car seats.

She ran inside as fast as her legs could carry her, bolted the back door, and ran upstairs into her bedroom, locking the door behind her. She stood leaning back against it for quite some time, listening to the hammering that was her heart.

Even with her fan roaring across the bedroom and all her security measures, it still took Kelly a long while to calm down enough to fall into something resembling sleep. And then it felt as if she had only been out for a few minutes before she was awakened by the phone ringing on the floor next to her bed.

She looked at the clock — it was almost midnight. Her hand shook with anticipation as she picked up the receiver.

"Hi," came the voice from the other end. "It's Rachel." Odd for her to identify herself like that, but in this case Kelly was glad she did. The connection was so scratchy she could barely hear anything on it.

"Where are you calling from?" Kelly asked. "This connection is horrible."

"Pay phone," Rachel said. "I guess it's this shredded cord. I'm not going to talk for long, though. I just wanted to tell you I think I saw Heather!"

"My sister?" Kelly said, the conversation moving too fast for her sleep-fogged brain. "Where?"

"I went to the movies with Sandy, and — "
Movies? Why didn't they invite me? was

Kelly's first thought. She was really hurt by this, but Rachel just blundered on as though there was nothing strange about her and Sandy going to the show together without even so much as asking Kelly along.

"Anyway, we were having pizza afterward, and — "

They went for pizza, too?

"And then afterward we were walking down Maple past the ice rink and out of the corner of my eye I saw this girl I could swear was Heather, and then she just slipped in the side door."

"Did she see you?"

"Don't think so. Anyway, she's still inside. I can see the entrance from here and she hasn't come back out."

"Will you wait there for me?"

"Can't. Got to get home. My mom's expecting me."

"I thought she was at your aunt's."

"She came back early."

Was Rachel's whole story about the aunt and having to stay home and baby-sit just a big concoction to cover for her and Sandy going out to the movies? On top of everything else that was going on, was Kelly going to have to worry that her best friend was finding a new best friend?

"Boy, your voice sounds weird," Kelly said.

"It's just this phone. I can barely hear you either."

"I guess I'll have to come down and check this out by myself. Isn't the rink closed for the summer?"

"I don't know," Rachel said. "Listen, I have to go. You'll be okay without me. I really think it's her, though, so hurry over before she goes."

"Right," Kelly said. But as excited as she was at the possibility of finding her sister, her intuition told her the situation she was walking into held dangers she couldn't quite see yet.

# Chapter 17

Kelly got dressed in a state of mild confusion. She couldn't find the sweatshirt she had just taken off when she went to bed. Noodle was hopping around like a furry madman and so she took him downstairs to let him out, then came back upstairs to find she had misplaced her running shoes. It was like one of those frustrating dreams in which she was trying to get to something and everything else was getting in the way, or she was running toward whatever it was through deep, thick mud.

These glitches and delays were maddening; she *had* to get to Heather before she left the ice rink.

At the same time she was rushing, though, she felt wrong about all of this, off balance. Why would Heather be here in Danube, hiding out? If she wanted to be here, it was because of everything and everyone she knew. Why would she run away and then just stay here? Or come back from California, but hide out once she got here? Was something wrong with her? Something she didn't want their parents to know about?

And what about Rachel? She had been so odd on the phone. It wasn't like her to lie to Kelly, or exclude her. Maybe this was about Griffin. Maybe, although she seemed to like him, Rachel secretly resented his intrusion into the summer internship that they had been planning to do together. Maybe she was hanging out with Sandy as some kind of retribution.

But this didn't really make sense. Over the years of their friendship, the two of them had developed ways of resolving any trouble that inevitably came up, and lying and not calling were *not* things they did to each other, even when one of them was angry.

Of course, everything seemed out of kilter lately. Unsettled and weird and scary. Luther still on the loose and the town in hiding. Although the curfew had been lifted and stores and restaurants and offices were open again, everyone went around with the black leopard in the back of their minds and at the edge of their peripheral vision. A town full of nerves on edge, and Kelly's were right up there among them.

She hated going out to the garage by herself in the dark, opening the side door, and groping around for the electric opener switch. She half expected Luther to jump down from the low rafters of the garage, or spring out from the backseat of her mother's car. Then, when she backed the car down the drive, she thought she saw Lonnie Bucks walking down the street toward her, but it was only her eyes playing tricks on her, and proved to be just a small tree.

Given her agitated state of mind, she really did not want to go snooping around a deserted ice rink at midnight, but what else could she do? If there was even a chance of finding her sister, it was worth putting her own jittery fears on hold.

When she pulled up in the parking lot, the ice rink didn't look just deserted, it looked abandoned. Windows were boarded up, sidewalks were cracked, frames for posters now displayed old remains — collages of torn off and overlapping pictures and words.

She got out of the car with some trepidation. The place looked so dead, she found it hard to believe it would be open, but the entrance door was ajar. She pulled it open and slipped into the darkness inside. Which was total. There wasn't a light anywhere. For at least a minute, she stood utterly still, just trying to get her bearings enough to take a next step one way or the other.

"Heather?" she said in something just above a whisper.

Nothing. The sound was blotted up by the dead, dark air inside here.

"Heather?" Louder this time, but still she got the same response. Nothing.

She put both hands on the wall next to her and began groping her way along. When she came to a door, she pulled on the handle and immediately felt a rush of frigid air. The rink! She was amazed that the ice was here in the summer. She had only been to this rink once, when she was ten or so, in the winter. She'd been a terrible skater, sliding across the ice on her ankles, then on her butt, almost never on the blades of the skates. One attempt had put an end to her dazzling skating career.

She would have thought the rink had been closed down for years, but apparently not. Apparently people still came here, even with the place in its decrepit state, even in summer. But not tonight, or at least not this late at night. The huge, high-ceilinged room she was walking into felt more deserted than any place she had ever been.

To make sure she didn't lock herself in, she felt around and grabbed a wooden folding chair and wedged it between the door and the frame on her way in.

"Heather?" she shouted lightly, then listened as the acoustics of air and ice magnified the sound a dozen times. Still there was no answer.

She took a few tentative steps to the edge of the rink.

"Heather?"

"Kelly?"

The reply was so faint and distant she couldn't really tell what direction it was coming from.

"Heather, is that you? Where are you?"

"Over here. Across the rink." It didn't sound quite like her sister; but then the voice was so faint and far off, it would have been hard to tell who it was at that range.

Kelly took a few tentative steps, trying to get closer, and right away was aware of the slippery ice beneath the soles of her shoes. Immediately she felt all the old terror she had experienced as a ten-year-old. She couldn't get her footing. As soon as she tried to move forward, her feet started sliding apart and she was sure she was going to fall.

148

"Heather?" she shouted. But this time there was no answer.

Then it got worse. She heard the door she had carefully propped open slam shut, immediately followed by the distinct sound of a bar being slid across the door on the other side.

She was locked inside.

Someone had tricked her.

The voice had *not* been her sister's.

Heather was *not* here, but someone else was.

From somewhere above her and off to the side, she heard the low, hoarse, vibrating growl of a large jungle cat.

She tried to run, but with every step she took, her feet slid farther apart from each other and her balance grew more unsteady. The growling grew closer and closer, echoing off the walls of the rink, finally breaking into a full-fledged roar as she tried to get some traction to run, and instead fell flat on her face.

Rolling over, warm blood flowing from her nose and from somewhere else — a cut on her head. She could sense it coming toward her. It? Luther? Whatever huge cat it was, whatever menacing jungle animal, the air was alive with its wild, fiendish, angry roar. A scream came pouring out of Kelly that matched the cat's in volume. And then she stopped and lay on the ice in total stillness and silence. And heard, sailing into this stillness and silence, the long *whoosh* of something flying down through the air.

And then she felt the claws.

# Chapter 18

At first, everything was a blur, then it went black again.

Time passed.

Then she woke up a second time, now into a fuzziness that gradually cleared.

"Am I dead?" Kelly asked whoever might be out there.

"No," came back a familiar voice. Rachel's.

Kelly tried to lift her head. "Oooo. Big mistake." She let her head sink back into the pile of pillows as she tried to bring everything into focus. Soon she could see that the face on the other side of the bed railing was Rachel's.

"Don't try to do too much too soon," Rachel said, taking her friend's hand. "How do you feel?"

Kelly moved her limbs, winced a little, then smiled as much as she could, "Not too bad, I guess, considering I expected to be dead."

"You've got a few stitches and you knocked yourself out falling on the ice, and they doped you up a bit last night so you could get some rest, but the docs say most of what's wrong with you is superficial. You'll be out of here in no time."

"Anything happen while I was away?" Kelly asked.

"Just that they captured Luther last night."

"Oh, wow. Did they kill him?"

"No, they got him with those tranquilizer darts. Hauled him back to the zoo."

"This was at the rink?"

"The rink? No. Why would you say that? They found him just before dark down in one of those caves by Hudson's Quarry out on the old Ash Road. He'd apparently been hiding out on everyone. Other than those two sheep he mauled, the only harm he did was to poor Sandy's arm."

"What about poor *me*?" Kelly wailed. "Don't I count?" Kelly lifted her bandaged arm and tried to peel it back a little to see underneath. Rachel slapped her hand lightly to keep her from poking around under there. She *was* worse than a parent sometimes.

"Well, seeing as that leopard was already safely back in its cage by the time you went to the ice rink, I'd say it was something else that got to you. What in creation were you *doing* over at that old place in the middle of the night anyway?"

"Well, looking for Heather, of course."

"What would your sister be doing here in town at the old ice rink?"

"Rachel, why are you even asking me this? You were the one who called to tell me that she was there."

"*What?*" Rachel said.

"Wait," Kelly said, putting a hand on her friend's arm. "Is it some mind-altering drug those docs gave me, or did I give myself a concussion out on that ice, because this conversation is making no sense at all."

"You? I'm beginning to think I'm the one with the concussion. First off, I didn't call you last night. I was gone almost all night. I had to go pick up my mother at my aunt Esther's, and didn't get home until about one-thirty. And then the hospital called."

"Ah," Kelly said. "So it wasn't you." She went on to relate the phone call she had received.

"I can't believe you fell for that," Rachel said. "Or that you believed I'd go for pizza and all that with Sandy and we wouldn't invite you. You are *so* paranoid and insecure."

"Thanks. It's always nice having an understanding and sympathetic visitor when you're in the hospital."

"Sorry," Rachel said, giving the top of Kelly's head an affectionate rub.

"Where is my family, anyway? Why aren't *they* here?"

"Oh," Rachel said, "that's a part I forgot to tell you. The police tried to get hold of them, but apparently they've left San Francisco. They think Heather might be in this cult up in the mountains and they're looking for her there. Anyway, even that detective says he can't reach them until they get back. So until then, I'm afraid *I* am your loving family."

"Oh no!" Kelly wailed.

"Do I hear a patient in need of rescue?" said a deep male voice coming into the room from the corridor.

"Griffin!" Kelly said, smiling, lifting her head, then putting it back on the pillows, gently this time. She was beginning to get used to the fact that she was a bit the worse for wear, and to know where her bruises were.

"What happened to you?" he said. "And whatever were you doing at that stupid ice rink?"

And so she had to go over everything for the second time.

"If you don't mind," he said when she was

done, "even though I'm not a medical professional, I'd like a look at that arm of yours." He nodded for Rachel to close the door to the room.

"Are you sure . . . ?" Rachel started to say, but he put a finger to his lips, then came back to the bed and began unwinding the bandage. When he was done, Kelly turned her head away.

"Argh. Sorry, but I can't stand the sight of gore, especially when it's *my* gore." But in the end, by the time they were done unraveling her bandage, Kelly felt compelled to look at her arm.

What the other two found themselves looking at *was* gruesome — a streak of five claw marks — but not as deep or vicious looking as the ones Sandy had received from the leopard. These were shallower.

"And notice how evenly spaced they are," Griffin said. "My guess is that if you put this mark next to the one on Melissa's locker, and the one in the dirt outside Kelly's window, you'd have exact matches."

"What are you saying?" Kelly asked, a little bewildered.

"I think someone let that leopard out of its cage, and it's the same person who made all the threats against the interns. Then, when the leopard ducked into that cave to hide for a few days and wasn't wreaking any havoc, this person decided to go on their own and impersonate the cat. Or make it seem as though other cats were being set loose, all to make a little more trouble — and trouble for *particular* people."

"Like?" Rachel said.

"Like people this person has it in for."

"But why?"

Griffin laughed. "Now you're asking me to get inside the deranged mind."

"But *who* is my question," Kelly said. "I want to find out who could be this big a creep."

"Dr. Hoffstadter, maybe," Rachel mused.

"Why Dr. H?" Griffin asked, and the girls had to explain, relating their adventure in the zoo.

"Wow," he said. "I can't let you two out of my sight for a minute. But what about Lonnie? That is, Lonnie and his mysterious black pet."

This time it was Rachel who gave the other two a question-mark look.

"Oh, I forgot you weren't there," Griffin said, and began detailing the events of the previous evening.

He was interrupted almost immediately by a nurse who came through the door, saw the unwound bandage on Kelly's arm, and said,

"What do you think you're doing? Out, all of you! I want this room cleared of all visitors immediately." And with that, she shooed Rachel and Griffin out of the room and went back to redress the wounds on Kelly's arm.

A couple of hours passed before the phone rang by Kelly's bedside. It was Rachel, with a plan.

"Start looking healthy," she said in a low voice. "I've got an idea, a plan to trap whoever did this to you. But I need your help."

"Why? What can I do?"

"Well, to be perfectly honest, you are going to be the bait in the trap."

# Chapter 19

Sandy and Jon stopped by to visit Kelly in the hospital, and she tried to act as though she felt a lot better than she actually did so the hospital staff coming in and out would think she was ready to be released.

Jon brought a kung fu poster as a present, and Sandy had a tin of Mexican cookies her mother had made.

"Oh, how nice," Kelly said. The two of them compared their matching arm bandages.

"We could start a support group," Kelly joked.

"Melissa said to tell you get well soon. She wanted to come, but says she hates hospitals and besides she has a haircut appointment this afternoon."

"I'm surprised she didn't just have her secretary call," Kelly said sarcastically.

When her friends had gone, one of the doctors came by.

"Does that hurt?" she asked. "I'm Doctor Benson."

"A little, but not much," Kelly said, smiling when she actually felt like wincing. But what else could she do? She couldn't lie around in bed when she was needed so badly at the zoo.

"Your temperature is normal, and so is your blood pressure," said Dr. Benson. "Still, we'd feel better if you hung out here for another day or two, just to be sure you're steady on your feet again. You had a bad scare in that ice rink, in addition to your physical injuries. Have you ever heard of post-traumatic stress syndrome?"

"No," Kelly admitted. "But I'm sure I don't have it. Mostly what I feel is itching to get out of here. Rarin' to go if you know what I mean." She flashed the doctor her brightest grin. Her "smile of good health."

She watched as the doctor looked at her carefully.

"Oh, all right then," Dr. Benson said. "I'm sure your mother can do about as much for you as we can at this point."

Not from the mountains of northern California, she can't, Kelly thought, but didn't say anything. Apparently her parents' absence hadn't made it onto her chart. *All right!*

She hopped out of bed, doing one of her greatest acting jobs of all time, which is to say not screaming when she shoved her injured arm into the sleeve of her sweatshirt, smiling broadly instead.

"Well, I'll be off now," she told the doctor.

"I hope the trip home won't be too taxing for you," the doctor said.

"Oh, I'm sure it won't," she said, truthfully in a sense because she wasn't *going* home. She looked down out the window of her hospital room and saw Rachel's car waiting.

Pam Perkins looked up as they entered her office.

"Kelly? You're out of the hospital already?"

"Pam, we have a plan to catch whoever has been doing all these evil things," Kelly said.

"And we need your help," Rachel told her.

The two girls spent the next half hour outlining what they had in mind.

"Whoever it is is after all the interns, but me in particular," Kelly said. "So Rachel thinks I need to be the bait in the trap."

"But now that Luther has been retrieved, won't the perpetrator be at a loss? I mean, while the leopard was missing, they could make it seem as though the cat was doing the damage. If everyone knows the cat has been caught, they can't work from behind that front."

"But when they scratched Melissa's locker door," Rachel said, "they were trying to make it look as though someone was letting out the other cats at night, too. Which, by the way, I don't think ever happened. But if we set the trap here at the zoo, they might think they can get away with it again. *So*? Do you think it will work?"

Pam chewed on the end of her pen for a moment, then said, "Maybe."

"Will you help us?"

"Well . . . it's true we all want to put an end to this before someone shuts the zoo down entirely. But I don't know . . . oh, this goes against my better judgment, but all right." She turned and looked directly at Kelly. "If you're sure you're up to it."

Kelly nodded and tapped her bandaged arm and bruised forehead. "Just a few scratches," she said, summoning up a toughness in her voice she didn't know was there. "I'll be fine."

"You will not be fine!" Griffin shouted across her kitchen at her. She had just outlined the plan for him. Pam had given them the go-ahead, and Kelly had just told Griffin, thinking he would naturally be in their corner. She hadn't expected him to go ballistic like this. "You will not be fine because you are not going to do this. I won't let you!"

"What do you mean you won't *let* me? Are you pulling some gorilla number on me? Excuse me, but I thought we only *worked* at a zoo, not that we were jungle animals. I thought we were liberated people of the late twentieth century."

"We are, and I am and you're right and all that," he said and smiled (the smile was still great, even when she was mad at him), "but you hit your head last night and I'm not sure you're thinking right now. And your parents aren't here, so someone has to be responsible for you."

"No. My head is fine and I'm perfectly capable of being responsible for myself. We have to catch whoever has been creating such mayhem, and this is the best plan to do that. Nearly foolproof, and safe, too."

"It's the *nearly* in that sentence that worries me," he said. "If anything happened to you . . ."

"Well, it's not going to."

"Well, it sure wouldn't if you stayed here

tonight and let me make you a soup dinner."

"Uh, would that involve your opening a red and white can?"

"*And* a box of saltines," he said with pride.

"Very tempting, but I'm afraid I really have to do this."

When he saw she was determined to go ahead with this, his smile evaporated.

"Well, good luck then," he said as he slammed out the back door, calling over his shoulder, "Maybe I'll see you again sometime when you're done being a superhero. Maybe."

She was furious. How dare he try to tell her what to do, even if it did come out of protectiveness and caring? If he was going to be close to her, he would have to let her make her own decisions. He would have to respect her as an equal. If he couldn't, then that great smile didn't amount to enough.

Only Kelly and Rachel and Griffin and Pam knew about the plan. They didn't know who the culprit was, and wanted to make sure whoever it was fell into their net.

"What's going on?" Jon said when he saw that Kelly had brought a sleeping bag to work with her.

"Ranger, the mountain lion, has some terrible infection in its teeth," Rachel explained.

"They're bringing a veterinary dentist down from Chicago," Kelly added, "but until he gets here, they need someone to spend the night with the cat, give him his antibiotics every two hours. And Lonnie is out of town getting a cheetah cub." A lie; Lonnie had merely gone home for the night, not knowing anything unusual was afoot. "So the duty kind of falls to us as the interns there. Rachel has to baby-sit her brother, but I can stay."

"Wow, you're braver than I'd be," he said, his fingers twitching over his face, as though searching out something to pick at.

"Yes," said Melissa. "What with everything that's happened to you, Kelly, and now staying all night in that creepy cat house. I just don't think I could do it either."

"All in a day's work," Kelly said, trying to seem casual about it. "No problem, really."

"Of course," Melissa said, pulling out her nail file, "your boyfriend will probably be by to help you through the night."

"I don't think so. He . . . uh . . . had to baby-sit his little brothers tonight."

She'd rather die than admit to Melissa that she and Griffin had had a fight.

"How sweet," Melissa said. "I myself am getting out of this jittery town entirely. *Ma mère* is taking me on a little shopping expedition, to Chicago. Have fun without me."

Even though she knew help was close at hand—that Pam and Rachel were nearby, along with zoo security guards — as she made up her cot and sleeping bag bed in the old, cavernous feeding room of the big cat house, Kelly felt extremely lonely and afraid. What if the situation got out of control and she was hurt again? Still, this seemed the only way to trap the person responsible for all this nastiness and pain. And no one would make better bait than she would. So although she was frightened, she also felt more crucial and central and important than she ever had.

The cats were pacing back and forth in their runs, active as they often were at nightfall, after a day of sunning themselves on a rock or shelf. She had gotten used to being around them, to their personalities, which were all very distinct. If she had set out to overcome her fear of large animals, she had partly succeeded, at least with some of the cats here.

Not with Luther, though. Even though he was still groggy from the tranquilizer darts they had shot at him to bring him in, everything about him, from his low, rumbling growl, to the coldness of his ice-blue stare, sent shivers of fear through her. As she lay down on her cot, turned off the lights, and tried to curl into the sleeping bag for the night, she kept her eyes wide open, staring into his cage, and was certain she could feel him staring back at her.

But in the rational part of her mind, she knew Luther was not the enemy she should be worrying about. Somewhere out there — probably quite close if they had heard she was here tonight "alone" — was the person who had made all the ugly threats against the interns, the person who let Luther out and then left claw marks of their own on Melissa's locker, in the dirt by Kelly's basement window, and on Kelly's arm. Whoever had done all this had to be a sick individual, and more frightening in a way than any jungle cat. You knew the worst a jungle cat would do — lunge and strike. But with this phantom, you had no idea what was up its sleeve next.

Everything was quiet — or as quiet as things get in a room filled with large cats — for the rest of the night. Kelly didn't sleep, but remarkably she did doze off a couple of times. At one o'clock, she got up and gave Ranger his fake antibiotics, pretending to fold it into a chunk of chopped meat, in case the phantom was watching.

When morning finally came, she didn't know whether she was disappointed or relieved that nothing had happened. She and Rachel talked with Pam in her office.

"Well, so much for that," Pam said. "Good try, Kelly."

"I still think it will work," Kelly said.

"What do you mean?" Pam said.

"My intuition tells me I should try it again. One more night. Whoever it is will come out tonight. I can feel it."

Pam sighed. "I don't know. I guess we can set it up again. Say that vet didn't get here. But I have to tell you I'm losing faith in this scheme."

Even Rachel looked at her funny, but Kelly stuck to her gut feeling. "Trust me," she said. "If my intuition — and my suspicion — are right, we'll catch our culprit before tomorrow morning."

That night, things didn't stay quiet and Kelly didn't have to wait long for hell to break loose. Soon after she had turned off the light and closed her eyes and evened out her breathing so anyone in the room with her would think she was sleeping, she heard the door open slowly. She kept her eyes shut and listened. One person. Light on their feet, not someone

tall or heavy. The person was moving very
slowly, but not so slowly that the cats didn't
notice. They began growling in a low, agitated
way. Kelly pretended to sleep on. The intruder was now halfway across the room toward Kelly's cot. Suddenly whoever it was
began moving very rapidly. Kelly could almost
feel the claws sinking into her flesh again. She
freaked out. Where were her rescuers?

And then, with what felt like an explosive
flash, the lights went on and two burly security
guards were wrestling the intruder to the
ground, loosening a grip on a five-tined gardening tool — the fake claws.

While the security guards held the squirming
intruder between them, Pam Perkins came in
with Rachel and ripped off the ski mask he
(she?) was wearing.

"Melissa?!" Kelly and Pam and Rachel all
shouted in overlapping voices.

Later, in Pam's office, Melissa sat in a
wooden chair, bent over and sobbing. Kelly
thought it was probably the first time she had
seen the real person behind the big phony front
Melissa had constructed. The nasty gardening
implement sat on Pam's desk, reminding them
all of everything Melissa had done.

"Here's your 'claw,'" said the security

guard as he nodded at the implement on Pam's desk.

"But why?" a clearly bewildered Pam asked Melissa.

"It's mostly about my father," she said between sobs. "I wanted to keep him out of trouble. He's been embezzling from the zoo for some time now. I think that's how we got so rich. I knew that big audit was coming up and if it did, everything he'd done would come out. I was hoping I could frighten everyone enough that they'd close the place down before the audit could happen. And . . ."

She stopped here, as though there was something more painful.

"And what?" Rachel prompted her.

"Well, I also guess I got pretty jealous of Kelly when Griffin started falling in love with her, and so I had my own reasons for wanting to get her out of the picture, at least away from the zoo. By focusing the attacks on her, I could kind of kill two birds with one stone.

"The first time, I just saw Lonnie's keys hanging on the wall in the feeding room and unlocked the leopard cage and pulled the door open a little. After that, I just took advantage of everyone being so nervous about big cats on the loose. I took that hand rake from our gardening shed, and I had made a tape of Luther one day. I just put the recorder on the floor of his habitat. When it was dark, with my rake and my tape, I was almost as scary as a real leopard. I put the marks outside Kelly's house, and on my own locker to take any suspicion off myself. And then I had my golden moment, faking Kelly out with that call, pretending I was Rachel, then luring her into the ice rink. My dad is part owner so I had access to his keys. The rest was easy.

"At first I was nervous about doing this stuff, but as I went along I think I got pretty good at it," she bragged as she looked around the room, and asked them all, "I scared a lot of people, didn't I?"

"You need help, Melissa," Pam said. "Very badly."

# Chapter 20

"What made you think one more night would do the trick?" Rachel asked Kelly. "What was that intuition of yours?"

"Well, it was partly intuition, and partly knowing Melissa was going to be up in Chicago that first night. I had my suspicions about her. The clues were beginning to add up."

Lonnie Bucks must have had a sixth sense about his cats. No one called him, but he turned up back at the zoo about the same time the police showed up.

"I knew somethin' was out of kilter. Felt it in my bones."

Kelly almost hugged him, she was so glad he hadn't turned out to be the bad guy in this. He stood and listened to every detail as Pam related them to him.

"Partly my fault, then," he said. "I was too

trusting of folks, keeping those cage keys up on the wall like that. Never thought anyone would be so wicked as to open one of the doors."

"But what about what you told us about cats needing their freedom?" Rachel said.

He looked at her as though he was trying to remember the conversation exactly, then said, "Well, that's in a perfect world. We don't live there. Cats don't have their freedom even in the wild anymore. People are hunting them, their land is shrinking. They don't have enough to eat or drink. Which is worse, I ask myself — that or this?" He gestured toward the zoo around them. "At least here they have me. I take care of them."

He turned to Kelly.

"Did you see me wavin' at you the other day?" he asked.

"Uh . . . well . . . I . . ."

"I seen you runnin' past and wanted you to meet my dog Homer. I was playin' fetch with the old boy. It's his favorite game. Labs are good fetchers."

So the big animal she'd seen him with had been a dog, not a jungle cat.

"Well, the truth is I wasn't sure it was you out there in the woods and my parents have always taught me, you know, the old thing about not stopping to talk with strangers. But I'm sorry I missed Homer. Maybe I'll run into you guys in the park sometime and we can toss him a Frisbee."

"I feel bad," he said. "Like you girls have gotten a bad impression of cats from all this."

"No," Kelly said honestly. "I've learned a little about cats through all this, and a lot about myself. I learned I'm a much braver person than I thought I was."

Dr. Hoffstadter came into the office as she was saying this, and said, "And it was your bravery, young lady, that is going to save this zoo from extinction. Along with my research."

It was the first time Kelly could remember seeing him smile. "Your research?" she said.

"Yes. On the effects of classical music on the temperament of primates. It's complicated. I don't think I could quite describe my methodology."

You don't have to, Dr. H, Kelly thought. And you never need know who was behind those Terminator and Frankenstein masks. Never.

She and Rachel laughed all the way to the car.

And when Rachel pulled the old Nova up into Kelly's driveway, she asked, "You need me to stay over tonight?"

Kelly had to crack up. "Well, thanks, but now that I've lived through the *Night of the Claw Marks by My Window* and the *Night at the Roller Rink*, I suppose I'll be able to sleep through tonight by myself, which I'm hoping is going to be the *Night That Nothing Happens*, now that Melissa's in custody."

"Weird, isn't it?" Rachel said. "Somebody you see every day and they seem normal — pretentious and pukey, but normal — and then they turn out to be psycho. I mean, that girl — forget her great clothes and all those CDs — she is going to reform school."

"And her father's probably going to prison."

"And maybe without him skimming all that money off the top, the zoo will recover and survive," Rachel said.

"Well, Wonder Woman . . ."

"Yes, Supergirl?"

"We did good for today."

Kelly got out of the car, went around and high-fived Rachel through the open car window, then went into the house.

She was on the phone ordering a pizza when the doorbell rang. She opened it to find Griffin holding a bouquet of flowers.

"Do these still hold clout for guys trying to apologize?"

"You think I'd be so easily swayed that I'd

fall for a dozen red roses?" she said.

"A dozen red roses obtained in the small town of Danube, Illinois, quite late at night after the two flower shops were long closed."

"Well, okay, maybe I'm a little impressed," she said, tugging him over the threshold by his sweater.

They held each other in the doorway for a minute. Then he said, "I was just so scared for you. And so I came off like some macho creep."

"Plus you thought I'm a girl and would mess up somehow."

"I did *not* think that," he said adamantly. "I already knew you're braver than I am. I was just reverting to type, and it's not even my type. Honest."

"Then, apology accepted."

"Can we do something tomorrow night?" he said. "I mean like a date? Something un-cat-related?"

"You've got a deal."

"Go to sleep," he said, kissing the top of her head, then loping down the walk to his car.

And she did. She slept a thick, deep, dreamless sleep for all the hours until the front door crashed open and her family came through — her whole family. Parents and luggage . . . and sister.

"Heather!" Kelly found herself yelling and getting her sister in a death-grip hug.

"Hey," Heather said, laughing, "don't kill me."

"I can't believe you're back," Kelly said. "And are you *really* back?" She looked at her sister and saw she was thinner and had clearly been through some hard times.

Heather nodded. "I got a little lost. There are lots of souls out there, all of them searching. And there are people who take advantage of that."

Kelly knew she would hear more later, when Heather was ready to talk. The important thing was her sister was home and it looked like she planned to stay.

"But enough about your sister," her mother said, shocked at Kelly's appearance, which she'd forgotten in the excitement. "What's this?" She touched the bandaged arm and pointed to the large bruise on Kelly's forehead.

These injuries seemed so far back in the adventure that she hadn't even thought to prepare lies about them, and so had to improvise with a long, excruciatingly dull story about working at the refreshment stand and a new spigot and a case of falling hot-dog buns. She made it sound like the sort of utterly uninteresting accident a sensible girl would have and kept going with the story until she had either lost or bored all of them. They needn't know they had Wonder Woman under their roof. Yet. She'd tell them sometime. For now, it was enough that she knew it.

# About the Author

Carmen Adams lives with her trained wolves — Pamela, Sharon, and Gladys — in a remote area on the northern coast of California where she writes, races motorcycles, and practices cliff diving.

*Point Horror*

Dare you read

# NIGHTMARE HALL

*Where college is a*
*scream!*

High on a hill overlooking Salem University
hidden in shadows and shrouded in mystery, sits
Nightingale Hall.

Nightmare Hall, the students call it.
Because that's where the terror began...
Don't miss these spine-tingling thrillers:

*The Silent Scream*
*The Roommate*
*Deadly Attraction*
*The Wish*
*The Scream Team*
*Guilty*
*Pretty Please*
*The Experiment*
*The Nightwalker*

# P●INT CRiME

*If you like Point Horror, you'll love Point Crime!*

A murder has been committed ...Whodunnit? Was it the arch rival, the mystery stranger or the best friend? An exciting series of crime novels, with tortuous plots and lots of suspects, designed to keep the reader guessing till the very last page.